LEAVE A REVIEW

AND TELL US WHAT YOU THINK.

IF YOU WANT TO STAY UPDATED ON THE PROJECT

PROGRESS, PUBLICATIONS, LIVE EVENTS, AND THE LIFE OF

AN AUTHOR

SUBSCRIBE TO MY NEWSLETTER

J.C. JUHL

Rift of Redemption

J.C. JUHL

Author: J.C. Juhl

Editor: Eleanor Laing

Publisher: Outcast Services

CHAPTER 1

With a flash, Raiden woke up, with hot sweat all over his icy cold body. It was another nightmare of the past, he realized. Every night, the nightmare would return. No matter if he saved his niece or got revenge. The nightmares and his feelings of guilt, regret, anger, and misery would never stop.

It took a moment before his mind settled down and he realized where he was. The fire had been put out a couple of hours ago, and he could see the bright stars in the night sky. There was no sign of fire or civilization in sight, but he knew that just a few miles beyond the hills lay the small town of Crossroads. He knew some festival was scheduled this time of year in the city, but that was not why he was going there.

To him, the only reason he needed to be in the town was because of a man named Ralph, who somehow knew the whereabouts of his niece, who had disappeared a year ago.

The complete story did not sound right, but it was a thing that had to be checked off the list of sources to make sure he did not miss any leads to where his niece was. A small tear came down his cheek as he thought about his niece and the rest of the family. Being gone during that event was worse than anything he had experienced or imagined before.

"I see you're up." Said Ariel, his sister-in-law, sitting over on a dead tree trunk and looking over the hills. Around her were a handful of stray cats, picking up crumbs she was throwing on the gravel in front of the tree trunk. No one knew why she was such a cat lover, but she was.

"Yeah, Captain Obvious." Raiden mumbles.

"I heard that," Ariel replied, throwing a handful of crumbs at Raiden's feet. Immediately, the group of cats ran over to get the food. Raiden jumped up in shock just as the cats dived for the food.

"What the Fuck." Raiden shouts.

"Another nightmare?" Ariel asked.

"Yes, another nightmare," Raiden said, with a feeling of loss in his mind.

"Maybe there is a spiritualist in Crossroads." Ariel had mentioned that before, and it felt like that was exactly what Raiden needed to help him keep moving forward on his mission. Raiden sat down on a block of broken cement, said in the old tales to be a part of a giant roadway that once crossed the entire land, now reduced to scattered pieces. Once he could sit down and close his eyes, both he and Ariel heard an explosion coming from the direction of the town they were heading for. His eyes immediately jerked open, and he looked over at Ariel. Even Ariel, who was sometimes rumored to be fearless, had a startled face. In just a second, Ariel and Raiden knew what they had to do. Ariel's equipment and supplies were still in her backpack, with her bow and quiver leaning against it. Ariel picked up and was ready to get to the Crossroads. She looked over her shoulders, seeing Raiden about done putting the blanket he was using as a pillow in his backpack. He quickly threw the straps over his shoulders, picked up his gun holster and belt with his handgun in it, put it on, then grabbed the rifle that lay next to him when he slept. Both started running towards the city to find out what was going on.

CHAPTER 2

It had been thirty minutes since they heard the first explosion, but now multiple explosions had gone off. With people across the town screaming, some in fear and others in genuine pain. With it just being Raiden and Ariel, they agreed they could have done nothing to help. Once they arrived over the hill, where they could see the city, they could see the group of Dynasty Knights standing guard at the main entry of the city. But why was the Shairyn army here? Raiden asked himself. This town was far out of the Shairyn Dynasty's ruling. From what Raiden understood, the town was under the Gateway's rule.

Raiden pointed at the group of Shairyn knights. Ariel knobbed, agreeing that they could not go in that way no matter what they did. Raiden and Ariel looked around the area to see if there was any other way in which they could sneak in.

Off to the side was a creek that ran under the metal wall that surrounded the town. The creek flowed into the town. Most towns had some source of water, and if it was a creek, they did not block it from getting into the town or from people in the town using it.

They both jogged over quietly to avoid confronting the Shairyn knights. The creek was down a hill, but once the entryway for the water was in sight, it was easy to tell that this town was running out of money. The metal bars that normally blocked people from sneaking in had been broken off. By poor people who sold the metal to help feed their families. Even in small towns, it was still where the rich had all they needed and more. And the poor were begging for food and help to survive. It was rumored that

Crossroads was as bad as Nova, the capital of the Shairyn Dynasty, when it came to greed and the harsh treatment of the poor.

They both squeezed between the bars that were left. They walked into the creek; around the creek, it was a small city park of some kind. But once they got in, there was a bridge crossing the creek into Crossroads, where they could hear soldiers. They quickly got out of the creek into the trees next to it, so they were not noticed. Ariel looked around to see if anything could help them figure out what was going on.

The knights were wearing their basic brown and tan combat armor with small devices on their shoulders, while they held their basic dynasty assault rifles. Those rifles were not like the ones that Raiden used, but were more laser or plasma weapons, and they were weapons only the dynasty was to have. In some towns of the flatlands, there was some technology, but never as advanced as the dynasties.

Raiden arrived next to Ariel and could see what she was watching. It looked like the Knights were gathering the people and moving them more into the center of the city. Raiden and Ariel slipped behind a few buildings, out of sight, into the dark alleys of the city. None of the Knights had been looking in the alleys. In them stood a handful of women, children, and the elderly. Raiden put a finger over his lips to signal to the group to stay quiet. They all shook their heads, yes, agreeing to stay quiet.

At the end of the group was a large man, wearing a pair of blue jeans, a tan t-shirt, and a bright blue ball cap with the letter C in a cherry red color on the front. No one had ever figured out what the logo with the letter C in red stood for, but it was a piece of treasure that his best friend Diego had found on one hunt for metal. Raiden, Ariel, and Diego had been on just a few years ago in the ancient windy city. Diego had a backpack just like Raiden's, with supplies and ammo on the ground next to him.

"Good to see you are still free," Raiden said to Diego. Diego just knobbed his head yes. Diego had been at a crossroads for a week ahead of Raiden and Ariel. He had gone to get supplies while Raiden and Ariel would find information about the man, Ralph, they had heard about, back in the town named Blue Grass. Which was a weird name since in the flatlands, there was barely even green grass.

"The knights are gathering people in the city square two blocks that way." Diego pointed down the alley. "Okay, do you know the outline of the city?" Raiden asked.

Diego shook his head yes. "Then you find the highest clear point you can and quickly set up there." Raiden commands. Diego knew what Raiden was talking about. Diego was a skilled long-distance shooter. The elderly called him Sniper back in his hometown, Sand Town. Diego took off to find his spot. Raiden and Ariel moved forward down the alley.

Raiden and Ariel move through the alleys slowly, stopping at the road crossings to check for the night traffic. Most people, besides the few who sneaked into the alleys, were gathered up in the main square of the town like Diego had said, surrounded by Shairyn knights. It was a block's distance from where they stood, but Ariel and Raiden could see that an old man was talking with the Knight in charge. Next to him and the Leading knight was a group of what looked like soldiers, on their knees with their hands tied behind their backs. Raiden hand motioned to Ariel that they needed to get closer to hear what was going on. Once they got close enough, behind the ruins of what the elderly called a library, with broken-up cement blocks around it. To Raiden's knowledge, the streets were back in the ancient days. From the stop, they could hear what was going on.

"Sir, these peasant actions are not the actions of the full community." As the old man pointed to the group of soldiers kneeling on the ground. They could hear some soldiers spit at the old man, talking in disgust at his comments. The old man just turned his head towards the soldiers with a glare of anger. They all quieted down and looked at the ground.

"It doesn't matter," the leading Knight said, looking around the square. It was like he was looking for some reaction from someone. "We are making you a sample of any community that stands against the Dynasty." The leader signaled his soldiers to open fire against the soldiers tied and kneeling on the ground. Raiden and Ariel knew it was now or never. Raiden walked out of the shadows while Ariel slid back into the darkness of the alley.

"Hello!" Raiden yelled to catch the attention of the Leader. The leader heard, looking over with a grin.

"Welcome. I was wondering when you would show up." The leader said, waving his hands, signaling the group of Knights to charge towards Raiden. Raiden lifted his hands in a position of surrender.

"You know it doesn't have to end this way," Raiden said with a smirk on his face. The Leader didn't fully understand why Raiden was talking like that. Raiden was outnumbered and had no chance of getting away. The lieutenant in charge of the mission to capture him would be pleased that Raiden was finally captured after all the chaos he had been causing for the last year.

The Shairyn Knights surrounded Raiden with their guns up and ready to fire. Raiden let them take his assault rifle and his handgun. They escorted him over to the Leader.

CHAPTER 3

It took Ariel a few minutes to get to her spot since she had to stay out of sight and make no extra noise while getting there. But she had made it there perfectly. She could see the group of Knights walking Raiden to the leader. It would be interesting to see how Raiden would distract the Knights and their leader.

Ariel scanned the town square. Noticing that only six knights had stayed to watch the soldiers and the civilians of the town. The civilians, unlike the captured soldiers, were standing against the back wall of the community center. Ariel had seen this position before. It was the basic position that knights would put people in before opening fire on them as a disciplinary execution.

Every time the knights did this, there were only a handful of survivors, and their duty was to make sure that other towns knew of this and understood this could happen to their town too, if they disobeyed the Dynasty.

She calculated her moves to take down the four knights guarding the soldiers, and she would have to depend on Diego to take down the two knights guarding the people. She had to wait long enough for Diego to set up position and for Raiden to get the full attention of the Knights. She waited for 10 minutes and could tell the talk Raiden was having was running out of time. That is when she saw the flicker of light on the roof of the tall general store. Diego was in position, and it was time to get into action.

Ariel took her bow and set aim with her only poison arrow left, and fired at one knight. In perfect timing, the arrow landed on the knight's shoulder and then burst into a bright green cloud. The cloud was big enough that it affected the other three knights standing close by. All their faces turned a sick color before they fell to the ground, making no sound. At the same time, the two Knights guarding the civilians had only microseconds before having the feeling of impact in their heads. The bullets from Diego's rifle pierced their heads. Entering one side of their heads and exiting out the other. Splattering blood across the grass as they both fell to the ground. The silencer of Diego's rifle worked perfectly, and the knights who were listening to Raiden noticed nothing.

With the light thump sound of the knights falling dead to the ground, the civilians were in shock at what was going on, but the soldiers were ready for action. Ariel ran over to the soldiers and started cutting the ropes that tied them together, freeing their hands.

It was a total group of only seven soldiers. After freeing the first six, the soldiers grabbed the assault rifles the knights had and set up position behind big cement flower pots and benches that were in the town square; The soldiers set an aim for the knights and the leader. "You get the people out of here and find cover," Ariel told the last soldier. He did as commanded and gathered the civilians, running them out of the town square.

As the vast group of civilians moved, a few Knights who surrounded Raiden heard something and turned around to see the people escaping. "Freeze!" the two knights yelled. And with that, Ariel gave the hand signal to the soldiers to open fire. Before most of the Knights had time to react, they felt bullets penetrate their armor. A few dropped instantly, while the rest, who were hit, were just wounded. But the ones wounded did not have time to put the plasma shields up because bullets sent from the rooftop by Diego took them down.

The leader and a handful of the knights who had not been hit put up their plasma shields to ricochet the bullets. The knights opened laser fire on the soldiers. Three Soldiers were down in a blink, and Ariel gave a verbal signal for the other three to retreat.

CHAPTER 4

Raiden saw it all happen and while one knight holding his weapons turned to see what was going on, Raiden gave him a sucker punch in the face and a quick kick in the side of his left knee to pop it out of position and put him in severe pain. The knight dropped to the ground in pain. But the Leader and other knights did not have time to react to Raiden.

Raiden grabbed his handgun and pulled the trigger, shooting the knight in front of him right in the back of his head. Raiden squatted down with a few bullets from the crossroad soldiers barely missing him. He grabbed his stuff, and just as he did, the Plasma shields of the other few Knights were up, guarding them from the gunfire. The leader stood behind the eight knights, still standing. Raiden was ready to open fire at the leader when he heard a few knights in the background running his way. It was time to get out of here, he thought to himself. He dodged off, out of Times Square, down one of the side streets, and now, he had to find the group.

How Ariel, Diego, and Raiden had worked together for over a decade. Raiden knew exactly where Diego and Ariel should be, but what about the civilians and other soldiers? He figured the soldiers who worked with Ariel would follow her, and then once Diego and he met up, the soldiers could let them know where the civilians and the other soldiers had gone.

The retreat places they would go would mostly be the last place they were not noticed and hidden, which was the alley five blocks from the city square with the civilians moving the other way, Raiden knew the Knights would either split which was a dangerous idea for them or gather in a safe spot and figure out their plan.

Raiden took around fifteen minutes to get to the spot, hiding from a few Knights who were moving down the streets to meet up with the rest at the city square. He had also seen some knights carry a Laser cannon that could take down buildings if they wanted to. He knew this might not all end well, but they had to try at least. Raiden came to the spot in the alley and, just as expected, there stood Ariel, Diego, and the last three soldiers.

"So, how do we find the civilians?" Raiden asked the Soldiers.

"At the city emergency bunker at the bank, six blocks from the town square." One soldier answered. Raiden understood, basic banks in most towns were not big or had much money, but they would almost always have an emergency or safety bunker in the building's basement. Some never used it, or it was just a creepy area, but all of them had a bunker.

"Take us there," Raiden told the soldier. "We need to set a guard so none of the Knights get close." The soldiers all knobbed yes in agreement that they had to take guard to prevent any of the knights from finding out where the people were hidden.

CHAPTER 5

2 hours later

Raiden, even being a positive-minded person, is full of energy. This day felt like it was going to end badly. Raiden could hear Ariel hold her breath, aiming towards the crowd of Knights.

While Ariel aimed, Raiden saw a Shairyn Knight out of Ariel's sight, aiming towards her. Wasting no time, Raiden dashed out from behind the crumbled brick wall, pulling the trigger of his Glock G23. The last three bullets of his clip fired off, hitting the knight, who was aiming at Ariel. The first two bullets hit the Knight in the arm and shoulder, and as the Knight flinched because of the pain, the last bullet was right into his chest, dead on, tunneling into his heart.

All the other Knights heard the sound and, for a split second, looked, but Ariel did not flinch. She released the arrow. This was one of the few arrows Ariel picked up at the last encounter with Shairyn's archers an hour ago. The arrow flew silently through the air and landed directly in the face of one of the Shairyn Knights. The knight collapsed to the ground, and none of the other knights looked beside one, who caught the blinking light on the stick of the arrow. Before being able to yell to warn his fellow knights, the arrowhead exploded.

Ariel had ducked behind one of the brick walls, and thankfully, Raiden caught the hint of what Ariel was doing and was behind the brick rubbish himself. Raiden did not know how many were killed or injured, but the cloud of dust and smoke gave him and Ariel a good opening to get to Diego.

A few buildings back, Diego was with a crowd of women and children. As Raiden and Ariel enter the building, two young men and a woman jump out in front of them, ready to swing their sledgehammers at them. Both Ariel and Raiden said the code and the young adults stood back and let them enter the building.

Diego was helping the last two soldiers who had been hit by the Shairyn knight's firearms but had not died. Ariel could tell this battle was not going well.

"How many people can still fight?" Ariel asked Diego. Before he answered Ariel, "What is that blood on your shoulder from?" Diego asked.

"Nothing. Are we at this ourselves, or do we have help?"

"Hold on, can you still use your arm with that injury?" Raiden asked.

"It is fine, you guys!" But as Ariel put her backpack on the ground and sat down in the chair to rest, Raiden and Diego saw her face in response to the pain she was in from the injury.

"No lying now, you're injured, Ariel. Get over here so the village doctor can help you." Diego said. From all the blood, Raiden knew she was out of the fight for now. And without a chance to respond, Diego pointed out, "I can help you, Raiden, but you know I have little skill in ground battle. I'm more long-distance and explosives."

"I know, but we both know I can't do this alone," Raiden replies.

Only seconds later, the young adults ran into the room. You could tell it was 200% fear in their eyes. But just as they got to the building, there was a rain shower of laser beams hitting them and the building itself.

Two of the young adults fell to the ground. You can hear their mothers screaming in sorrow in the background. The last one could get behind the wall before the bullets hit them. But Ariel, Diego, and Raiden knew it was a now-or-never point in the battle. Ariel grabbed the grenades she had hidden in her backpack. She pulled the pins of a few and threw them out the door as far as she could. It hit the ground, and they all could hear a knight shout out, "Grenades!!!" and the rest of the crowd of knights tried to jump behind the walls. When the grenades exploded, it was hard to tell how many they hit, but you could tell at least three Knights now had battle injuries.

Both Ariel and Raiden looked out the door to get a quick glimpse of what was going on, but before getting a full view, beams hit the walls they were hiding behind.

"EVERYONE OUT OF HERE NOW!!!" Raiden shouts. The women, children, and men ran out of the front area and deeper into what the ancients called a warehouse. Raiden then looked over at Ariel and Diego. All of them said a phrase from one of the ancient tales they heard as children. "All for one and one for all!" The three shouted.

CHAPTER 6

1 Year Earlier

The sun was high and hot in the sky, with no clouds for the day and most of this whole last week. Raiden could feel the sweat running down his forehead. Even with his hat, t-shirt, and jeans, he felt like his head and whole body were on fire. It would only be another couple of minutes before they fully made it into the ruins of the ancient city and its shade from the giant towers. People from across the world would explore the ancient cities to find rare artifacts and some of the rich collectibles they could sell.

But Raiden, Diego, and Ariel were there for the metal, and any other material they could trade for gold and supplies at the Flatland trade center, which was nicknamed The Arsenal. It lay on an island in the middle of a river they call the mud river. The crew walked into what was once thought to be the big city, but is now just ruins. It was said before the final war that there was water next to the city, which was once called the Great Lakes. Now, however, a desert-like expanse of dried dirt extends for hundreds of miles. It takes a 2 2-week-long trip to get to a water source that was controlled by the Shairyn Dynasty in the City of Nova.

The ancient city's name was written in a unique language, which most people in the world nowadays don't understand. But Diego did and was good at interpreting what was written in the ancient city. There were crumbling towers everywhere in the city. Raiden looked at the map that they had created for the city. It showed that around a few more ancient buildings, they would be entering an unknown part of the city they had not yet explored.

Many people hunted in the city, but could only stay for so long because of the sandstorms created by the winds. This city had tales from old folks of once being called the Windy City. Some mutant raiders occupied the city and would ambush people and take their money and supplies. Normally, killing them in the end.

Arial Shouted, "I found one of the metal ruins."

Diego and Raiden ran over to Ariel. It was some bent round metal and sticks of metal pointing out of the ground.

"Is that it?" Raiden asked, looking a little puzzled.

"I think so. There is a story about there being art sculptures made of bronze all around the Windy City. But no one had found them yet."

"Diego, get your shovel, and you and I will start digging. Ariel, you watch guard, to make sure no savages surprise us."

"Okay," Ariel replies.

Raiden and Diego started digging and digging. The more they dug, the more of the old statues they found. After the bombing of the Final War, the statues were in pieces, but enough that this was profitable for Ariel, Diego, and Raiden. With Diego's strength, he could easily pull the sled behind him. And with this much bronze, they might even be able to send someone back to the outpost on the edge of the city to buy a mule.

By the time the shadows of the Ruined towers fell over the city, they had plenty of bronze and needed a mule now, which they could afford.

"Who is taking watch first tonight?" Raiden asked.

"I will watch until midnight," Ariel replies.

"Ok, that works. I will take over after that. Diego, get as much sleep as you can. We will need your strength tomorrow." Raiden said, knowing Diego was a 6-foot-tall, heavily built man of pure muscle.

Raiden took his blankets out of his backpack and put one on the ground to protect himself from the sand fleas and the other as a pillow.

Diego replied while yawning, "Sounds good to me." It didn't take long before Diego's blankets were set up, and he was snoring.

Hours later, around midnight, Ariel softly pushed her foot against Raiden's chest. She had to do it twice before Raiden woke up. He had to shake his head a little to wake up and get rid of the sand that blew onto him because of the windy city's wind.

Once Raiden was up and standing, Ariel handed him the pistol she had.

"Where did you get that?" Raiden asked.

"I have had it in my backpack this whole time," Ariel replies.

Raiden nob told her to get some sleep. Ariel agreed and sat down. In a cross-legged position, which Raiden's older family members called "sitting in the Indian position". Ariel was different. Raiden could never figure out if she were sleeping or meditating. Her breathing was deep and soft either way, and she was in action the millisecond something moved or made a noise.

Raiden walked around, looking into the dark. He wasn't a mutant, but he had better night vision than the average person. The sky was dark with stars, and a beautiful view of the full moon. The wind blew, and Raiden could hear the sand blowing with it. Raiden noticed a slight movement down the road. He stood still and listened to hear any noise. He heard soft voices speaking the language of the Windy City that he didn't understand, but he knew the only people who spoke that language were the mutant raiders who robbed and killed adventurers and explorers.

Raiden kneeled and snapped his fingers. Ariel immediately woke up. She looked at Raiden, who was pointing towards drifts of sand, and then hand-signalled invasion. Ariel picked up her bow and arrow. She slowly moved over towards a drift by the fallen tower on the other side of the pathway. It looked like no raider saw her move. She got into position and took out the fire ignition arrow. Aimed up in the sky at the right angle to have the arrow land right between the drift. She looked over at Raiden, and he gave her the hand gesture to shoot.

Ariel shot the arrow up, and it came back, as expected, behind the drifts. Ariel had set a timer on the package for 5 seconds. About 15 feet above the ground, the arrow sprayed out fluid all over the ground, covering a 20-foot circle, and then once the arrow hit the ground, there were small sparkles of light. Then the ground burst into flames.

Once it happened, Raiden and Ariel immediately heard the raiders screaming in pain. 5 ran out past the drifts into the open on fire. Other men started shooting, not knowing where the arrow came from and giving away their positions. The 6 other Raiders were scattered around the pathway, but most were in plain sight of Ariel. Ariel took out some normal arrows and took her shots. She took down two other raiders before they realized where she was.

They turned around and opened fire on Ariel with some guns, but not the basic guns; they were made of scrap, which affected the accuracy of the bullets. No bullet came close to hitting Ariel, but she still dropped behind the sand drift she was by. The surrounding sand was shooting up after every bullet hit the ground. She hand signaled Raiden that she was down for now. Raiden shook his head, and now it was his turn.

Raiden saw the location from which most of the bullets were coming. It looked like they were everywhere. If he moved out, Raiden would be in plain sight. Raiden scanned the area and saw an opening into the ancient tower by him. It was in the building's corner and looked like it was a tall, wide window without glass. He figured he should be able to sneak in and get behind the raiders. Raiden quickly got through the window. Inside, he was in a spacious room, which reminded him of what was called office space in the old tales. He could easily tell those raiders had been there before.

There was a doorway that went into the rest of the building. Once through the door, the rest of the building had barely any walls to separate the offices. It was wide open. Raiden listened and heard the raiders talking in their native language. Raiden was sure they were planning on charging towards Ariel soon. He sprinted down the floor of the building to a part of the building with an outside wall all broken down, as if a vehicle had crashed through it. Old vehicles had complete blocks of metal in the front, and some towers had underground chambers with an unbelievable number of vehicles in them. Complete treasures for metal hunters.

Raiden slowed down and was quiet as he approached the opening. He peeked out and saw the back of one raider. The raider was wearing a leather chest piece for armor over a t-shirt. The leather armor must have been made of coyote skins. There was fur on the shoulders, with some spikes made of metal sticking out. It looked like the raider was wearing jeans and a helmet made of metal, with artwork on the side. The rest of the raiders were wearing similar armor. Once this battle was over, if they survived, Raiden knew they would make a little more money.

The raider was getting ready to stand up. That was the signal for Raiden. He took his hunting knife and jumped out of the building. Once on the ground right behind the raider, he took his left hand like lightning around the head of the raider and pulled back. Before the raider could do anything, he took his right hand with the knife, slicing it across the throat of the raider. With no noise, the raider dropped to their knees and held their hands to their neck as blood rushed out all over the sand. It only took seconds before the raider was dead on the ground, just bleeding the last of its blood.

Raiden picked up the gun and a combat knife. Looked and saw another raider reloading its gun as it was aiming towards the drift; Ariel was behind. Raiden took the combat knife and threw it at the raider. It landed in the back of the raider, slicing through their armor. The raider tried to scream in pain, but spat up blood. This means that Raiden did as he wanted and punctured the right lung of the raider from the back.

The other Raiders didn't notice and started shooting and walking towards the sand drift, and Ariel was behind. Raiden ran over to the wounded raider, took his hunting knife, and split the raider's throat. Before the body hit the ground, he took the combat knife out of the raider's back and threw it again. This time, it only flew by the raider. Leaving a cut on its jacket. Raider stopped shooting and looked around, making the rest stop and look back too, but before they could do anything, Raiden used the scrap gun that he picked up from the first raider he killed and opened fire on the rest.

2 of the 4 raiders left were hit immediately, scattering blood everywhere as their bodies were ripped up and they fell to the ground, dead. The last two raiders realized what had happened and started running in the opposite direction of Raiden and Ariel,

towards the camp. As the raiders passed, Diego still lay there sleeping. Ariel shot two arrows, both hitting each of the raiders in the back and puncturing them. The arrowheads burst out of the chest of the raiders, with blood bursting out and raining on the ground. The raiders dropped to their knees, then lay flat on their faces next to Diego, who had just woken up.

"Took you long enough," Raiden said while laughing. Diego looked around and saw the bodies next to him in the sand. "What the hell happened here?" he asked.

"I will explain later, but we need to round the bodies up and get them away from the camp. We don't need to battle coyotes, too.".

It took a few hours to clean up the mess that was made during the battle. Diego had found the camp, equipment, and sled that the raiders had brought to take back what they would have stolen. It was perfect because now they didn't need to get one sled. There were beef jerky, nuts, leather bags of water, other weapons, 53 silver pieces, and more scrap metal that the raiders had stolen. Along with 15 mules to help move the sled. It was a 100% treasure for them.

They took as much as they could on the sled. They put the naked bodies of the raiders in a pile and set the pile on fire. The disgusting smell it made was horrible to be around, but the three left early after this, and it wasn't their problem.

They started their journey back home as they passed out of the ancient city. Raiden looked back at the city ruins. To him, the towers were still amazing, even if they were falling apart. In the legends, it was once a wonderful place until the final war. He turned his head back and joined the crew in the week-and-a-half-long walk back to the arsenal. To Raiden, this was a brief adventure, and it will be great to get home and see the family.

CHAPTER 7

The black, heavily armored, steam-run Shairyn supply train entered Sand Town late in the afternoon. To them, this was a small town in the middle of nowhere, but it was by requirement every couple of months that a crew of a Major, first lieutenant, a few sergeants, and a large group of privates would visit some of the small villages out in the forbidden flats and gather information on the natives and collect taxes, along with the team picking up supplies and material to be taken back to Nova.

The emperor of the Shairyn dynasty had been waiting for weeks to receive supplies needed to manufacture and upgrade more weapons and armor for the invasion of the Republic. The Republic comprised many towns and cities and combined their number of supplies, army, and independence, making it a problem for the dynasty. The Dynasty wasn't sure, but it was rumored that the Republic was becoming close allies with Gateway. A giant ancient town that didn't become ruins but a thriving business, that controlled the muddy river, most of the southern part of the continent on which the Dynasty was on. Gateway was also one of the Dynasty's worst enemies, making it soon. The Republic and Gateway together would be a full threat to the Dynasty.

Upon reaching the town center, most of the crew signaled the group to halt. The major called up one sergeant and told him to take his crew of 10 privates and collect taxes from the local town hall and the small businesses in the town.

The Major would go talk to the leader of the town and set up the trade pickup. The first lieutenant and the rest of the sergeants would gather supplies, book housing, and a dinner for the privates while they stayed in town for the night. Sergeant James ordered a group of six privates to come with him to get the supplies. Sergeant Anderson ordered two privates to follow him over to the local saloon to get the dinner set up. And the rest of the privates were ordered to go to the local warehouse to stay till dinner.

Private Jefferson and his friends followed orders to the warehouse to wait for further commands from the major. Most soldiers knew Private Jefferson as Lucifer because of his normal attitude and behavior outside of his hours of duty. The other privates had heard the elderly tell tales, even though most nations, dynasties, and kingdoms had outlawed the book they came from, about an evil character called Lucifer. The book with those stories had been around in the ancient years, but had been banished after the final war. Nowadays, most people do not understand what happened in the final war or why the ancient book was banished. To the privates and most people for the last millennium, the book was known as the forbidden book. The soldiers believed the nickname Lucifer fit Private Jefferson perfectly.

Sergeant Smith and the privates march to the warehouse to stay for the night. A couple of hours later, the Major and Lieutenant returned to the warehouse. As the Major and Lieutenant enter the warehouse, a soldier notices them coming through the door and shouts out, "Salute!". All other privates quickly stand up, put their right hand on their heart, and bow their heads. The Lieutenant said, "Still," loud enough for all soldiers to hear.

All the soldiers lowered their arms, putting them by their sides, and stood up still. In a calm voice, "The city will have the material and money ready in two days. I will give you the next two days off to rest and relax. Dinner will be ready at the saloon in another hour." The Lieutenant then points out, "I will need 6 soldiers for watch-on-guard shifts?" All the privates knew this was for them, and by volunteering, they would get some more time for pleasure once they returned to Nova, compared to the rest of the soldiers. Even extra pay if the Major was in a good mood when they returned to Nova.

Six soldiers raise their hands quicker than the rest, and the Lieutenant points at them, "Follow me." And starts walking back to the door. The Major turns back, looking at the rest of the privates, and said "Rest.". All the privates and three sergeants relax and go back to what they were doing.

CHAPTER 8

As the hour fades away, Lucifer gathers his six favorite fellow privates, Robinson, Wilson, Barrett, Charles, and Griffin. The ones that kiss his ass and will do about anything for him. The group walks to the saloon, making jokes and looking at some of the local women, making faces that gave out a vibe to the women that the answer no, didn't matter to them.

When Lucifer and the crew passed the general store, Private Charles saw a woman looking like she was in her early thirties, with a summer skirt on, long legs, and beautiful green eyes from what he could see. Private Charles stopped and whistled. The group stopped, and Lucifer turned his head to see what the private was referring to.

Lucifer looked over, seeing the attractive woman. To Lucifer, she was a treasure, and if taken, it would be a genuine show-off to the crew. Lucifer tapped Private Charles's shoulder, lowered his head just enough to Charles's ear, and whispered: "Watch".

Lucifer walked over with a grin on his face. He walked up to the lady and smacked her in the ass as he got in front of her.

"Nice ass, young lady." He knew she was older, but still being called young to most women was a compliment Lucifer felt. "Want to honor a warrior tonight?" he asked.

He could see she was startled because of his actions. But to him, it didn't matter.

In a calm, faint voice, she replied, "Sorry, but I need to get home before it is dark and feed my children." Lucifer could see the fear in her eyes and a slight shake in her hands.

"You know you owe me for protecting this town, you and your family!" Lucifer said, grabbing her arm and pulling her closer.

"Saying no is disrespectful, honey," Lucifer said with an evil grin on his face. In Lucifer's mind, she was a no matter what now. Suddenly, Lucifer felt an object smacking into his shoulder, bouncing off, and hitting the ground. He quickly swung around to see what was happening, pushing the lady and making her fall to the ground. Not too far away, by the corner of the building, a young teenage boy, probably around 14, stood prepared to throw another rock at Lucifer.

With no hesitation, Lucifer asked, "What do you think you're doing, little shit?"

"Get away from my mom!" the teenager yelled.

Lucifer could tell the boy did not realize until it was too late that Lucifer was a soldier and what Lucifer's strength might be if they fought. Lucifer could see the fear in the boy's eyes. But with no hesitation, the boy threw another rock, hitting Lucifer in the chest. This time Lucifer felt it, and he was sure it would leave a bruise. Lucifer moved quickly over to the boy, ready to give the boy a lesson on throwing rocks at a soldier. He quickly grabbed the boy by his shirt before he could throw another rock. Lifting him and shaking him. As the lady shouted out, "I am sorry! Don't hurt him, I will go with you!" Lucifer didn't care what she said now.

"YOU'RE GOING TO LEARN NOT TO DISRESPECT A SOLDIER, YOU LITTLE SHIT!". Before Lucifer could throw him to the ground and show the boy what he meant. One of Lucifer's friends shouted out, "Lucifer!".

Lucifer quickly turned around to see what was up. There, Lucifer saw the Major exit the hotel where he was staying. Along with other people getting out of the stores and houses to see what was going on. Lucifer dropped the boy to the ground, saying,

"I'll see you later, little shit."

Lucifer passed by the lady, who was still on the ground with tears in her eyes.

"You're lucky bitch." He said while he spat on the ground at the lady's feet. Lucifer and the privates continued their path to the saloon.

CHAPTER 9

Later that night, after dinner, and the Major, Lieutenant, and sergeants, along with most of the other privates, had gone back to where they were sleeping for the night, Lucifer still sat at the bar with a whiskey bottle. Lucifer took his last drink out of the bottle and looked down the bar at the bartender.

The bartender could tell whatever was going to happen next would not be good. Lucifer had had plenty of shots and time to come up with some strong resentment towards the boy and mother, and some nasty plans on how to make them pay for what they did earlier that day, after giving the bartender a nasty look.

"Get over here," Lucifer commands.

"Need another, sir?" the bartender asked, trying to stay away from Lucifer as long as possible.

"Just get over here!"

The bartender walked over, taking his time, hoping someone in charge was still there, and heard the drunk private being rude. But no one in charge was still at the bar, considering how late it was.

"You know who they are!" Lucifer shouts.

"Sir, I don't know what you are talking about." The bartender answered.

Lucifer grabbed the bartender by the shirt, pulling him down to the top of the bar.

"Bullshit!" Lucifer shouts and then asked, "Who the fuck were they?"

"I am telling you, sir, I don't know." The bartender answered.

With a wicked face, Lucifer looked at the bartender. "One last chance, asshole." Pulling out his hunting knife. "You are dead if you lie one more time." A smirk plays on Lucifer's lips as he says.

The sweat coming down the bartender's forehead told Lucifer that the bartender was horrified and believed everything he was telling him.

"Okay! Okay! Sorry, I'll tell you." The bartender said in a panic of anxiety,

"Who was it? And where do they live?" Lucifer asked one last time.

"They live out of town in a small house, North of here." The bartender replied.

"Good. Who's all home?" Lucifer asked the bartender while looking at him with evil eyes of anger.

"Just Marlena, her son, and daughter?" the bartender replied in a fearful voice.

"No, father or farm help?" Lucifer asked.

"No, sir, her brother is out of town still." The bartender said with tears in his eyes, and with a low whimpering voice, "Please don't hurt them. It was just a mistake. It won't happen again. I promise you. They will stay out of town till you leave." The bartender said.

"I don't give a fuck!" Lucifer replies.

Lucifer pushed the bartender back with enough force that he fell to the floor.

Lucifer shouts out, "Get over here!". Charles, Robinson, and Griffin heard him immediately and said, "Hey!" to Johnson, Wilson, and Barrett to get their attention.

They all look over at the other three with an expression on their faces.

"Lucifer wants us, you idiots," Charles shouts.

All three reply, "Shit!"

The group walked over to Lucifer. Charles asked, "What's up, Lucifer?"

"We show that bitch and little shit. Why don't you respect soldiers?"

Wilson replies, "You sure, Lucifer? We are all drunk, and you know the Major won't approve of it."

"Screw major. This is personal and not his problem."

Wilson replied in a hesitant voice, "Okay, I'll help."

"Good," Lucifer said, then looking at the bartender, who had moved to the other end of the bar. "You don't say shit or you're dead, you understand?"

The bartender shook his head yes. Looking to see if anyone had heard anything, but all there was a local drunk who had his head on top of the bar counter, sleeping. The only thought going through the bartender's head as Lucifer and the other privates left the bar was, What have I done?

CHAPTER 10

Marlena woke up to a loud barking. It was late at night; all the animals should've been in the barns or coop and safe. The coyotes or wolves should not be close, Marlena felt, but the dog was still barking. This meant Marlena needed to go out and see what was happening.

As Marlena left the house to see what was happening, Robert awoke to the sound of the door. What? Is Mom outside? Why would she go out this late? Robert thought to himself.

This made Robert nervous, and he needed to go out and find out what was going on.

Marlena walked out the front door with an old handgun, or what the elderly called a pistol, that Raiden had found on his one trip to the ancient ruins called Hartford of the West. The family only had two dozen more bullets left. Raiden, even being on dozens of trips since he had found it, had not yet found any more bullets that worked with it.

As Marlena looked around to see what was causing the dog to bark. She did not realize it had gone silent. Before anything clicked in Marlena's head, Johnson and Griffin grabbed her from behind. They held her back with her arms in position, with the gun only pointing at the ground. Lucifer walked out of the shadows, followed by the other four soldiers.

Lucifer took the gun out of Marlena's hands and threw it to the side.

"You won't be needing that," Lucifer said as he moved his right hand up her side, then over to her breast, giving a little squeeze, and then up to her neck, where he put his hand into a choking position. Lucifer closed his hand a little, blocking the air flow.

"You fucked up," Lucifer said while taking his hand off her neck, standing back a few steps, and slapping her across the face, hitting her left cheek.

After recovering from the slap, Marlena spat on Lucifer's face. She knew it was over for her, but the kids could still get away. She deep down knew Raiden and the crew would take care of the kids.

Lucifer took a rag out of his pocket, using it to wipe the spit off his face. "Shut her up." He said, pointing at Wilson. Who jogged up with a piece of cloth? Wilson wrapped the cloth around Marlena's face, preventing her from yelling or warning her children.

"Take her back there," Lucifer said, pointing back toward the moon's shadow of the barn. "Do as you please, then kill her." Referring to Johnson and Griffin. Marlena tried to scream, but there was no sound because of the cloth.

"You guys," Lucifer said while pointing at Charles, Barrett, Wilson, and Robinson, "check the barns for any stash of gold, silver, or goods we can use."

Lucifer turned around to go back to the horse. The other men started heading to the barns and sheds. Robert had seen the entire event and knew his mother was in great danger along with him and his sister, too, if the soldiers weren't stopped. He looked around to see if there was anything he could do to help. Lying in the weeds, not too far off the side of the door in the gravel, was the pistol his mom had tried to use.

This was his only chance. Robert had never used a gun of any kind. His uncle Raiden had taught him how to use a bow and arrow and a crossbow. But that was all Raiden had taught him. The bow and arrows were in a locker inside the house. Using the gun was his only chance to save his mom, Robert felt.

Robert walked down the stairs to the house's first floor in the living room. He made no noise through the living room, then out the front door, and quietly moved towards the gun. Not making noise for the privates to hear while sneaking through the gravel.

Once he could pick up the gun, he grabbed it and was ready to aim and shoot at Lucifer. He had to save the family, Robert thought.

CHAPTER 11

Lucifer stood watching as his two friends assaulted Marlena. Completely ripping off her nightgown. Lucifer understood she was attractive, and the pleasure might be worth it to the men, but to him, after what she and her son had done that day, she was not worth his time anymore and deserved this. Even though the men were his friends, their actions such as this were what made the difference between him and his friends. They were only going to be private with no chance of promotion. While he, on the other hand, had the potential for more in his military career, he thought.

But where was her son? He was the one who deserved to be tortured and killed the most. Not his mother. Lucifer ground his teeth together as anger and resentment filled his mind. Lucifer turned away from the two privates with Marlena and started to look and see what the other privates were doing and if they had found anything worth taking. He could hear Privates Charles, Wilson, and Barrett in the buildings and saw Robinson walking out of the shed empty-handed. Lucifer waved his hands to flag Robinson to come over to him.

When Robinson arrived, "Burn the house down." Lucifer commands.

"Yes, Sir," Robinson replies. Lucifer's friends always acted like he was more than just a private; he was more like a sergeant to them. The one in charge.

As Robinson moved past Lucifer, heading to the house. They all heard a gunshot, and Robinson screamed in pain as a bullet smashed right into his knee. Shattering it into small pieces, and blood was going everywhere. Some even splattered on Lucifer's uniform, who stood just a foot away from him.

Robert moved forward out of the shadows, and the three other men ran out of the barn. Robert straightened his aim at Lucifer, ready to fire again and hopefully hit him this time. Robert shouted out, "Let her go!"

Just as Lucifer moved forward, Robert pulled the trigger again. The two men with Robert's mom threw her to the ground and pulled out their guns, aiming at Robert.

Before the other men could fire their weapons, Lucifer held up his hand to let them know not to fire. They were all puzzled about why. But Lucifer had heard it jam and recognized the weapon. Knowing it as a Zip 22LR. It was one of his collectibles he had gotten from the Generals as an award of Honor for the battle of Silvis, where the Shairyn Dynasty conquered the Milba Kingdom located in what the local storytellers called the Appalachian Mountains. He had saved ten of his fellow crew soldiers. Lucifer knew Zip 22LRs would stall constantly when fired and could see that Robert was trying to get it to work.

Tears streamed down Marlena's face as she tried to scream, "Run, Robert!!!" But with a rope around her face, no one heard her, especially not Robert.

"Good job, young man, unless you were aiming at me," Lucifer said with an evil grin on his face, knowing his revenge would be soon.

Robert saw Lucifer moving forward with no gun in his hands, but Robert knew it was not good. "I told you to stay back!" Robert said, pulling the trigger again, but it clicked. The trigger remained jammed. Robert shook it to help fix the jam, but no difference. He stared at it, trying to figure out how his uncle would unjam the gun.

"You know Private Robinson will die soon or have to be amputated and kicked out of the army," Lucifer said while looking over at Robinson, who was waving to get one soldier to help him. But no one else was going to move until Lucifer told them to.

"Being able to shoot makes you a great recruit for the Shairyn Military," Lucifer said. Robert was shivering and ready to just take off running away in fear. He could not, he thought. His mom and sister needed him.

Robert looked at the gun again. This time, he saw the part that might jam the gun. Robert quickly did what needed to be done and swung the gun up to shoot again, and this time kill Lucifer.

As Robert swung the gun, he did not notice that Lucifer was already within arm's reach. As Roberts's arm swung up, Lucifer caught his arm in motion and quickly twisted it. Sending severe pain up Robert's arm. Robert screamed in pain, dropping the gun to the ground. Lucifer let go of Robert's arm and grabbed him by the shirt collar, pulling him close up and whispering in his ear, "Your sister's and mother's deaths are your fault." Then, he smashed his right hand with an army knife that every soldier had into Roberts's chest just far enough away from Roberts's heart that he did not die instantly.

Lucifer let go of Robert's collar, and Robert dropped to his knees for a few seconds, with the knife still in his chest, then fell into the dusty gravel. The darkness of death was slowly fading over Robert's eyes, and with the last chance to see anything, Robert saw

Lucifer wave at the men by the barn, signaling them and saying in a few words to kill Robert's family. The last thought and the feeling before the darkness fully took over, Robert felt the extreme guilt of what he believed was his fault now.

CHAPTER 12

Marlena saw Robert fall to the ground. She could feel the tears running down her cheeks. But she had to get help. She ran as fast as she could with tears running out of her eyes in sorrow as she ran into the field of weeds, not seeing the pieces of the broken fence Raiden was going to get rid of when he returned from his hunt.

Marlena tripped on the wooden ruins of the fence. Falling into the weeds face first. Marlena was dizzy and almost unconscious, but as her mind returned to normal, the fear again spread through her body. She got up as quickly as she could, but once standing up, Griffin tackled her to the ground. Hitting the ground, this time into a bed of rocks, she could feel her skin break on her forehead, and pain coming from her arm as if it had been broken.

She tried to scream in pain, but she still had a rope around her face. Blood was dripping down from her forehead. Before even getting the chance to move again, Johnson pulled up and stood behind her while Griffin got back up. Johnson grabbed her forehead and pulled it back towards him. Then quickly, with no thought or feeling of remorse, Johnson slid an army knife blade across her throat. Blood flooded out of her throat from her jugular veins. The blood splattered everywhere, even on Griffin.

Johnson released his grip on Marlena as the blood fell down her chest. Marlena's body fell to the ground, landing on the rocks. Her blood splattered all over the rocks.

Griffin yells, "WHAT THE FUCK!!"

Johnson just giggled and walked away.

"What, you didn't want some pussy? You're a piece of shit."

Griffin yells.

"We do not have time. Didn't you hear the orders?"

"What orders?"

"Lucifer wants us to search the house for any other residents and take any gold or silver we find," Johnson replies.

CHAPTER 13

The scene was gruesome for Jessica as she stood looking out the living room window. Jessica cried in sorrow and horror at what could happen now. She had only been back to visit for a week to learn a little about running a family. Jessica's true love, Ken, proposed only a month ago. She held her hands over her mouth to help block the sound of her crying. Tears flooded out of Jennifer, but knew she had to suck it up as her little brother always said when trying to show off. She had to get out of there now. Before she left the living room for the kitchen, a bottle with a rag coming out of the bottle on fire crashed through the front window, scattering glass across the living room floor.

Jessica jumped, diving into the kitchen as the alcohol spilled over the living room. Flames burst, spreading across the living room in seconds. The fire was making thick smoke that spread through the house. Jessica stayed on the floor but could feel the smoke getting thicker and filling the house quickly.

Another bottle crashed through the back windows by the back door, blocking all doors to leave the house. There was only one way to get away from the flames for the moment. There was an opening in the floor in a closet close to the back porch that her mother used to stash valuable belongings like gold and silver coins or iron ingots and other metals.

Jennifer crawled over and pushed the wood they used for their fire away from the closet, and under the wood was the small opening into what her uncle called the treasure spot. Jennifer pulled the wooden floor square up, throwing it across the room. Hitting the floor loudly. She moved into the underground space, hearing one of the soldiers' yells, "Did you hear that?"

She lowered herself into the opening. The area she had lowered herself into was much smaller than she had thought. To move anywhere, she was going to have to do what her uncle, Raiden, called commando crawling. As she started to commando crawl, she could see the stash of small bags of coins and the pile of iron ingots, copper, and even a small ingot of silver. Right now, metal and coins are not part of her goal, she thought.

It was dark in the treasure spot. Jessica could barely see anything, but the flames from above were shining through the floor, and she felt the heat as it got hotter and hotter in the small space.

With little light, she still saw a small line on the wall at the edge of the area. She crawled over, and once at the spot, she could see a small piece of wall that was the opening outside. There were no door hinges or door locks. She pushed it out quietly, trying to make sure the soldiers heard nothing. Once it was completely open and the piece of wood was flat on the ground, Jessica looked out slowly to make sure no one saw her. No soldier was in sight. She could hear them on the other side of the house. It sounded like they were starting fires in all the barns and sheds, with the farm animals screaming.

Once she was fully out of the treasure spot, she stood up and looked around to see if there was anywhere she could go. She saw that prairie on each of the crop fields west of the farm. The fire was now all over the house, and flames were even spreading through the treasure spot. She sprinted to the field. She knew once she was far enough in the field and prairie because of the flames, she could disappear into the shadows.

Jessica sprinted as far as possible into the prairie. Once the farm was in the far distance, where it was just a spot of light on the horizon, she stopped to see where she was. It looked to her like she was miles into the prairie, close to the Love Blood River.

Jessica knew she could find help in a small neighboring village close to the Love Blood River. But she felt exhausted, out of energy, and light-headed from breathing in too much smoke and the adrenaline in her body wearing off. Once she moved fast again, the lightheadedness turned into her collapsing to the ground. While falling to the ground, she heard in the far distance wolves howling,

giving the signal that prey was in the field and it was time to hunt.

CHAPTER 14

A group of men heard the wolf howl. They knew some wolf's hide, teeth, and claws would sell well at the next dock they stopped at.

"Captain." One man whispered, kneeling and looking at the prairie from behind a log of wood, from the many fallen trees between the river and the prairie. The captain moved over to the man's side to see what was happening. The man pointed out into the prairie. In the far distance, a couple of miles away, there was a small glow on the horizon of a fire burning.

"I saw someone drop out there." The man said, pointing at the top of a small hill. "I am sure that is where the wolves are going."

To the captain, if someone or some other animal fell and was hurt, it would be the perfect prey for the wolf pack. The captain waved at the rest of the small group of men. They moved over in the darkness at their best to not make noise. The last thing they wanted was for the wolves to know they were sneaking up. The captain raised his hand to have the group halt the movement. He signaled two of the five men who were with him to split up and circle around and meet the rest in the middle.

As the captain and his crew approached the spot, they could hear wolves approaching. It wasn't long before the wolves growled. He halted the men, hoping they were not the reason for the growling. But then he heard a cry and then shouted, "Get out of here!" and then a louder growl and barks followed. The captain heard a man in the far distance, toward the house on fire, shout out. "She's over here.".

The captain knew they needed to be quick and get the wolves before the people arrived. The captain was confident that the four people would lose, but he felt it would be a waste of bullets and time. They needed to leave before dawn. They had a long trip to get to the Big Easy and trade in the material on their boat for some good money.

The captain looked up over the tall prairie grass and saw a group of around four people with torches moving in their direction. "Let's hurry this up. Get the wolves and the person." The men looked puzzled at the order, but followed through.

The men moved slowly until they could see some wolves who surrounded a young woman. Three of the men who had old rifles took aim at the pack of wolves. All three pulled the trigger simultaneously. Three wolves fell to the ground, and one howled, alarming the rest to take off. The three men set out again to fire again, but the captain said, "We've got to go." And they lowered their rifles.

The two men who circled around came into the open area. They grabbed two of the dead wolves, and one rifleman grabbed the third. The captain came into the clearing and saw the young woman on the ground. The captain could see the terror and fear in her eyes. "Do you want to stay here or come with me?" the captain asked. "Or do you want the people who burned your farm to help?" For a split second, he even saw more terror in her eyes.

"Please help." She whimpered, and the captain signaled for the other two men to help her up. He could tell she was weak and needed to rest to recover.

The captain took one of the men's rifles and aimed out into the prairie, looking to see where the people were. He saw the group of people who were following the young lady retreating to the burning farm. The captain turned and joined his men on the trail back to where their boat was docked on the Love Blood River. They would let her recover, and then they would find a way for her to pay them back for saving her life.

CHAPTER 15

Raiden and the crew arrived at the Arsenal after the month-long trip. Raiden was walking in front with Ariel next to him and Diego back a little, leading the pack of mules. It was a basic business day at the Arsenal. You had your basic cattle crew taking the cattle to the auction house to be auctioned off, and some cattle taken to the local butcher. To be turned into food for the cattle crew and sold to the local community.

Even with it being a busy weekday in town, Raiden was noticing something, and it did not feel good to him.

"Ariel," Raiden said, to grab her attention.

Ariel replies, "What's up?" already getting the vibe from Raiden's voice that something was bothering him.

"I don't know why, but something isn't right?"

"What gives you that idea?" Ariel asked.

"Well, no one says hi or even tries to sell us something. You know, we always get bombarded with salespeople when we get back from our hunt," Raiden replies.

Ariel had not thought of that, given how she rarely dealt with them. That was more than what Raiden did. He was the man in charge.

"I didn't notice, but we can ask Neptune when we get inside."

The crew saw the sign to Neptune's Shop from a far distance. The building was a big storefront, with almost six other shops all across the front of the building, but that was disguised for the public. All six of the other shops were fake and were never opened, but were owned by Neptune. But most of the public did not know that. The building looked run down, out of shape, and falling apart. It was wooden with a brown darkness coloring to it; in parts of the wall and window frames, you saw rotten wood as a disguise. Raiden signaled Diego to go over to the local stable and stand guard, watching over the mule and all the metal that they had found in the Windy City.

The front door to the shop they were going to enter was a solid steel door, which was worth a lot of money if it could be stolen and was just out of place in a run-down building like this. Raiden and Ariel walked up to the door. Raiden stopped for a second, looking around, still not feeling comfortable. Without hesitation, Ariel knocked on the metal door. The sound stunned Raiden.

"What the hell?"

"I don't know what's going on with you, but I want my money," Ariel said in a tone of voice. That made Raiden know she wanted to get this over with because she hated Neptune. Ariel knew Neptune liked her because of how she treated her, and the treatment was not polite.

A ringing sound went off, and a click. That was the sign that the door was unlocked, and they could come in. Ariel opened the door. Once they walked into the building, it was a whole new view. The walls around the building were all metal, not wood. The wood siding was just camouflaged on the outside of the building.

It was a giant open building. They were standing on top of the staircase that went down two stories. In the big accessible area, you could see the giant tanks of clean filtered water that Neptune had. She sold tanks of water a day to small towns to help people and farmers raise their cattle. From Raiden's understanding of water, it looked like Neptune still had a month of clean water. Alongside the tanks of water were what Neptune calls shipping containers full of scrap metal. Neptune was the only person who had a connection to the capital of Nova, where the water supply came from, because of how polluted all the other sources of water were in this region..

Raiden looked around to see where Neptune was. After a quick scan, he noticed her waving at them to come down the stairs to her office. As they walked down the stairs, a gateway door on the far side of the building opened, and you could see the mud river and a river barge getting into position to dock up and get loaded with the scrap metal. They had just gotten back in time, Raiden thought to himself. It would take another couple of hours to load the barge, and that was plenty of time for Raiden to sell the metal to Neptune.

CHAPTER 16

Raiden sat in a chair next to the office door with Ariel to his right in a duplicate chair. Neptune sat in her large leather business chair and stared at Ariel. Neptune was dressed in light blue jeans and a red blouse with a replica of an ancient hat. The hat was bright blue with a light red C in the middle. Neptune was drawn to Ariel. Ariel felt as if she was being stared at. She hated the bullshit way Neptune treated her. It was obvious to Ariel that Neptune had the hots for her. But this needs to be over and to break the silence and get the meeting over with, Raiden opened the conversation.

'We have real bronze."

"You, do you?' Replied Neptune.

"Yes, we do. Around 5000 pounds of bronze and a herd of 15 mules."

Neptune's eyes widened, with a greedy smile coming across her face. Raiden knew now was the time to bargain because even though Neptune paid the best and was the most connected to Nova, she was not the only one he could sell to; the others would pay well, too. This much bronze would put that salesperson on the Shairyn Dynasty's radar for needed resources.

"I am willing to give you 100 gold and 25 silver."

Raiden interrupted Neptune before she finished her sentence.

"Bullshit. I am no idiot, and neither are you. You know that much bronze is worth more than that in gold and silver."

Ariel stood up immediately and waved at Raiden.

"Let's go. I know someone who will pay better." She said.

Raiden got out of the chair, and Ariel opened the door.

"OK, Hold. I am sorry. Let's talk a little more." Neptune said.

Raiden looked over at Ariel, and she shrugged her shoulders with an expression of your choice. Raiden sat back down, and Ariel followed his actions.

"One last chance or we are finding someone else," Raiden said with a smirky grin, knowing if any other store got an offer, Neptune was screwed, and this situation was checkmate now.

"Since this is 5,000 lb. of bronze and 15 mules, I am willing to offer 900 gold coins, 300 silver coins, and your choice of supplies to take home to your family."

Raiden looked with a smile at Ariel, and she smiled back. Good money, they both thought. This was enough money to last a couple of years, not counting them hunting again and the family selling farm products later this year, too.

Raiden leaned forward, sticking his hand out, and Neptune did the same, and they shook hands.

"Deal," Raiden said, and Neptune replied the same.

"Give me a second to get the gold and silver. Let my workers get the Bronze into the building."

They both nodded their heads. Neptune got up and walked out the door. Once the door closed, Ariel said to Raiden.

"Let's go make sure there is no foul play."

They both hurried up the stairs and out the door. Ariel whistled, and Diego replied, whistling back. Signaling that help was needed. Ariel and Raiden ran over to the barn. When they walked in, they saw some of the workers trying to get to the wagon on which the bronze was. Before there was a chance, Ariel threw a dagger, slamming right into the wall in front of one worker. With how close the dagger was to the worker's face, it was obvious why he was startled and jumped back. Raiden turned his head around and looked at Ariel. She was already ready to throw another dagger, and this time to hit a worker.

Raiden waved his hand down, signaling Ariel to put the dagger back. When Raiden turned back to talk to the workers, he could see the anger on their faces. Before the fight began, Neptune stepped into the barn, saying. "I was wondering where you went." With a fake smile. It was easy for Raiden to tell that she was disappointed that this little plan did not work and that she was going to have to fully pay now.

Raiden nods his head at Ariel, telling her to get her dagger and go stand by Diego. He walked over to Neptune. She had brought a large, thick leather bag with the money in it. She handed it over with a frown on her face. Raiden said to Diego. 'I need your help, Diego."

Diego walked over and took the bag, carrying it over to the closest workbench in the Barn to count it. The workers moved, and Ariel put her hand on another one of the six daggers she had on her knife belt across her waist. They understood to just wait.

It took Diego a few minutes to fully count the coins.

"We're good," Diego shouts.

"We'll go pick out the supplies. We just need a letter with your permission," Raiden said.

Neptune pulled out a piece of paper with an even bigger frown on her face. Raiden took the certified piece of paper and waved at Ariel and Diego.

"Let's get supplies and then head home."

"I'll get the mules and wagon out once it is unloaded," Diego replies.

"I'll guard the money." Ariel points out.

"Okay, see you in a little," Raiden said as he walked past the group of workers, moving the large pieces of bronze metal from the wagon. He could see the annoyed faces of the workers and saw Neptune standing by the door into the office with a disappointed face. Raiden showed a grin as he walked out the door. In a couple of hours, they would be on their way home, and it would be a while before metal hunting would need to be done again.

CHAPTER 17

It had been a couple of days since they had received the money and supplies from Neptune. It would only be a few minutes before they reached Sand Town, a small town at the edge of the flatlands. The town had been abandoned for centuries until a group of people from Nova moved into the area to get away from the capital.

The town had only two hundred people with train tracks running through it. It sat on top of a hill that overlooked the flatland, which once was a healthy prairie, with tales of there once being farmland as far as the eye could see surrounding it. Nowadays, it is close to a desert because of the heat and lack of rain. The Shairyn dynasty army used the train rails to transport supplies to Nova. The army would travel around the flatlands from settlement to settlement to pick up the supplies they were owed. They did not take the normal roads that people traveled on. Sand Town comprised around forty-six houses and a few businesses. Such as a barber shop, a Saloon, a small doctor's office, and a local supply store,

The crew was going to stop in town, some get haircuts, others get drinking supplies to celebrate, and Raiden was going to stop at the local supply store and sell half of the supplies he got from Neptune for free to Jason, the owner, at a dirt-cheap price.,, That way, the town depended less on outer resources and the supplies would be at discount prices for the people.

As Raiden entered the little general store, it looked normal. Daily supplies were there on the shelves. He could see the binder on the counter where you filled out paper for the store to order supplies, or round them up in the store if they had them. On the counter by the register were small glass bottles with candy sticks in them. The small bell was on the counter, and Raiden rang it to get Jason's attention. Raiden figured he was in the back, counting supplies and filling out orders to send to nearby farms. When Jason came up front and looked to see who was at the counter, Raiden saw Jason's face of startlement, making Raiden think something horrible was going on in town.

"I am so sorry, Raiden. We wish we could have done something." Jason said.

"What are you talking about? We just got back."

Before Jason answered, Ariel and Diego came in.

"What are you all doing? I thought you had stuff to do?" Raiden asked.

Ariel replies, "Something is not right."

"Everyone is giving us this look," Diego said.

Raiden turned to Jason. "Spill the beans, what is going on?" but Jason hesitated to speak.

Raiden slammed his fist on the countertop. "What the fuck is going on?"

"Your farm is gone. Your Nephew and Sister are dead, and your niece Jessica is missing."

"What?" Raiden said. "You're joking, right?"

"No, I am not. I am so sorry." Tears were running down Jason's face. Raiden believed him now. But wanted proof. Raiden turned to Ariel and Diego.

"Find the doctor NOW!"

Ariel and Diego shook their heads yes and took off toward the doctor's office. The Doctor would be the one who dealt with the bodies. He was the doctor and the undertaker of the town.

Raiden sat on the steps to catch his breath. He still did not think it was true. Jason must be mistaken about what he is talking about. Raiden figured that while Ariel and Diego found out what was happening, he would step into the saloon and wait.

A couple of hours went by, and Ariel and Diego still had not returned. The saloon was small, with only a few tables and a bar. One window and a front door. It was dark inside, and it felt right to Raiden. It was out in the flatlands, so the shot cups were glass but worn down, you could tell. The ale that Raiden was drinking came out of wooden pints that the local craftsmen made. Raiden was on his 10th shot of tequila and his 12th pint of ale. The bartender never hesitated to fill up his drink. A few people came to say they were sorry for his loss, but they did not come over until he was already drunk, and Raiden told them to go away. After that, everyone stayed away.

At first, when Ariel came into the bar, she did not see Raiden. He was usually at a specific table where he and his family sat every time. But he was not there this time. Ariel scanned the bar to see where he was. Over in the corner at the end of the bar, away from everybody, sat Raiden.

She walked over to Raiden and sat next to him.
"You're late." He said.

"I know," Ariel replies. She frowned and patted his back. "Diego and I checked it out, and it is true. I am sorry, Raiden."

Raiden slammed his glass to the counter, then picked it up and threw it across the bar.

"FUCK!" he yelled as tears came down his face.

"What happened?" Raiden asked.

"Sorry, Raiden, but we are not talking about it while you are drunk."

"Fuck you, yes we are." Raiden said, giving off a face of anger at Ariel, "What the fuck happened?" he said, with tires coming down his checks.

"We are going to Diego's first. You need some rest," She replied.

Without a word or any hesitation, Raiden jumped up and swung at Ariel. But he was slow and clumsy because he was drunk. Ariel quickly moved out of the way, and Raiden missed, in the process, losing his balance. He fell to the floor like a heavy object. Raiden tried to get back up, but could not. The ale and tequila finally affected him. Ariel helped him up and walked him to the door. Once at the door, Raiden swung again, trying to hit Ariel and missing. He stumbled forward but did not fall. He turned around ready to try again, but Ariel had enough of his drunk ass bullshit. Her first swing hit Raiden on the side of his face, right on the left cheek. The perfect knockout punch. Raiden fell backward onto the bar floor, out cold.

CHAPTER 18

The pain on Raiden's face was intense when he woke up the next morning. All he remembered was Jason saying something horrible and then someone knocking him out cold at the bar. But what did Jason say that was so bad, and who hit him? He thought.

Ariel walked into the room. Raiden had not realized it, but he was not home. He was at Diego's house, but why?

"How are you feeling?" Ariel asked.

"Okay, I guess." Raiden touched his face and felt the pain, like he was going to have a bruise or something.

"What happened last night?"

"You got drunk and swung. I knocked you out and took you to Diego's."

"What the fuck?" Raiden said, with a confused look on his face.

"You were drunk, no shame," Ariel said with a grin on her face, putting a cup of coffee on the nightstand next to the bed.

Raiden picked it up and took a sip, said, "Yeah, thanks." The headache was severe, and the bruise on his face was hurting.

"Why did I get drunk?" he asked.

"You don't remember, do you?" Ariel asked, with a frown on her face.

"I guess not. What's going on?" It slowly came back to his mind on what had happened, and tears started, and the memories of yesterday were coming back.

"Your sister and nephew were murdered a couple of weeks ago," Ariel said. Making it so that the nightmare was true, and it was not a horrible dream.

"What? Oh shit, I remember. What about Jessica? Is she ok?"

"Sorry, she is missing. We did a hunt, but her trail faded away once we got to the mud river. Whoever had her must have taken off on a boat."

"Damn it," Raiden said with frustration. Ariel could tell Raiden's temperature was rising.

"Cool off, Raiden. We have yet to know the complete story." Ariel said. "We need to go into town and talk to some people."

"No one said anything yet?" Raiden asked with an angry face.

"Jason, the store owner, was talking, but you interrupted him and sent us out to get information. And like I said, you got drunk." Ariel answers.

"Ok, we will have to go into town then," Raiden said, and Ariel pointed out. "Yes, but watch your temperature. The Marshall is back from bounty hunting." Raiden knew now he needed to cool off. The Marshall did not like Raiden, anyway. Starting a fight or any violence would not end well.

"Okay, I understand."

Raiden sat up on the edge of the bed with tears starting again. He shook his head a little and wiped the tears off his cheeks with his hand. He was already dressed but covered in dust because Ariel dragged him to Diego's after being knocked out cold; he assumed.

"Hey, good morning, bro," Diego said, waving at Raiden to come and sit down at the counter.

"I got food if you need any."

"Thanks, but I am good," Raiden replies. Raiden could hear Diego's kids in the background playing outside and his wife doing something in the living room. He felt the peace flowing through the house and wished he could feel this again with his own family.

"Join me if you feel like it. I got to find some stuff out." Raiden got up and started for the door. Ariel got up and followed.

"Are you coming, Diego?" Raiden asked.

"Oh, I guess," Diego said as he put the food on the table. Ariel and Raiden waited at the door as the kids came flying in straight to the table. His wife walked in and gave him a kiss on the cheek, said, "You'd better get going, honey." Diego smiled, remembering he had the best wife he could have asked for. They left ready to get the

information they needed. However, they had to.

CHAPTER 19

Raiden and his friends arrived back in town around 9:30 am. The store opened about an hour ago, and the daily business of the town was in motion. They rode the horses to the shop. They all got off, took the reins, and put them around the rails on the hitching post in front of the store. Raiden signaled Diego to stand outside to watch out for the Marshall. If the Marshall showed up, he would be on Raiden's ass to calm down and go back to Diego's. Calling it a

Marshall's investigation. Raiden knew he would say hell no to that, and chaos would break loose after that.

Raiden and Ariel walked into the store, catching Jason filling the shelves with the new shipments of supplies. Jason looked up and noticed the bell on top of the door ringing. Right away, Raiden could tell Jason was nervous.

"Hey, Jason," Raiden said in a calm voice, while Ariel walked over to the shelves, looking at supplies.

"We did not finish our talk yesterday. I figured I'd stop here before getting to the doctor's office."

"Oh, Okay. How may I help?"

"Well, yesterday you said something about my loss. What were you referring to?'

"I am sorry, but I do not remember. It must not have been important." Jason turned around and walked to the door to the back. Said, "I need to close. I have to go home and check on some stuff. You can come back later."

A few steps after turning around, a dagger flew by Jason's face and hit the wall next to him.

"Not so fast," Ariel said.

"I asked what was going on," Raiden said, this time with an angry face.

"I am sorry, I'm sorry." Jason was shivering. "All I know is that the month pickup crew was in town. A private nicknamed Lucifer picked up some supplies with a few friends and walked out. He ran into Marlana and Robert."

"So, what happened?"

"He said some inappropriate words and was hitting on Marlana. It looked like he was going to assault her." The fury adds up in Raiden.

"Hey Raiden, remember Jason is the messenger and is letting us know. He did nothing wrong." Ariel said.

"I know, I know, sorry Jason. Anything else?"

"Well, while I was looking through the window, and before Lucifer put a hand on Marlana, your nephew Robert threw rocks at him. The reason nothing happened there was because the Major of the squad walked outside to smoke from the hotel."

"So somehow this guy killed them," Raiden asked.

"Yes, that is the rumor in town," Jason replies.

Raiden was about ready to punch something, and Jason pointed out before it happened, "No one knows the full story."

"Does the Marshall know anything?" Arial asked.

"He was here earlier asking the same questions."

Raiden thought about it for a second, then asked Jason, "Do you have any clue who all died?"

"Marlena and Robert. Jessica is missing." Jason answers.

"Does anyone have a clue what had happened to her? The tracks go to the mud river and vanish?" Ariel asked.

"Nope," Jason replies. "The Marshall believes it was one of the trade crews from over east. They were shady, and the Marshall made them stay out of town." That sounded reliable to Raiden. Some of the eastern trade crews would do anything for money. Kidnapping people to trade for money was one of the massive things they would do.

"What were they doing around here? Why weren't they at the arsenal?"

"No one knows. They showed up wanting to stay in town. Marshall would not let them." Jason pointed out.

"How long were they here, and when did they leave?" Ariel asked.

"It seemed like they were here a couple of days before Marshall left for his theft hunting. They stayed till Nova soldiers showed up, and your house was on fire."

"How long ago did this happen?" Ariel asked, since Raiden was catching his breath because of how frustrated he was.

"About a week ago," Jason replies.

"Okay, thanks. Sorry about the bullshit." Raiden flipped one of the gold coins he had gotten from the metal hunt onto the countertop. Jason's eyes went wide when he realized what it was. Without a second wasted, Jason swiped it up and replied. "No problem, I am still open later if you want to sell me some supplies you got from the arsenal."

"Will do," Raiden replies.

Ariel walked over to the counter, reached over, and grabbed the jagger from the wall. "I apologize, too. Did not mean to scare you." She said with a grin on her face.

Raiden and Ariel walked outside to meet Diego. They looked around for any sign of the Marshall. But there was no sign. He must have still been in the office snoozing. Raiden looked at Diego. "It was one of the Nova soldiers. Just a private, we believe."

"Shit," Diego replies.

"We need to ask around if anyone knows where Jessica is," Raiden said.

"How did they find your home?" Diego asked.

"Good Question?" Ariel replies.

"Since you already talked to the doctor. I want you to talk around town and find out where my sister and the kids lived. I will go to the doctor's office." Raiden said.

"You sure you want to do that alone?" Diego asked.

"I am good. You guys just find out how?" Ariel and Diego both nodded their heads yes and turned around, heading over to the local bar. Raiden took off towards the doctor's office.

CHAPTER 20

Raiden got to the local doctor's office. It was a small two-story building, old, made of sturdy oak, with only two windows and the front door looking out at the street. Raiden read the sign above the door and said, "Sand Town Medical." This doctor and medical office had been in Sand Town for over 3 decades. Raiden opened the front door and walked in. Inside was a small waiting room with a desk by the doorway that led to the rest of the building. At the desk, the nurse Beth sat reading the local bi-weekly newspaper called The Times. The newspaper had been around for centuries, as far as everyone knew. No one had ever figured out why they called it the Times. It sounded weird. The rumor was that it was what ancient people called it, but no one besides the people in charge of the newspaper knew. It was the newspaper's big secret.

As Raiden walked in the front door, the bell rang. Raiden said, "Good morning." To the nurse at the front desk. She laid the paper down and looked up. She quickly realized it was Raiden.

"I am so Sorry," she said.

"It's okay," Raiden said back.

"I will get the doctor right away," Beth said and swiftly got up and went through the door next to the desk. In a few minutes, the doctor came through. He walked up to Raiden and stuck his hand out for a handshake. Raiden did the same to be respectful. But then the doctor pulled Raiden in, giving Raiden a deep hug, and patted him on the back and said politely, "I am so sorry. I could not believe what happened."

"Thanks, Doc, I can't either," Raiden replied, with a small tear coming out of his eye. The doctor turned around and started towards the door. "Call me Adam and follow me."

Raiden and Adam started walking down the hall, passing Adam's office and record room, and then into the exam and processing room. Two embalming tables sat in the middle of the room. Adam had multiple types of tables, which were all in the supply closet on the other side of the room, but this was the table for anything that had to do with dead bodies. There was a sheet over both bodies to hide the identity till the family arrived. Raiden could tell by the size of the bodies which one was his sister and which one was his nephew.

Adam walked over to the table where Raiden's sister's body was located. Before Adam lifted the sheet, he asked Raiden, "Are you ready for this?"

Raiden nodded his head yes. Tears came down Raiden's cheeks when Adam lifted the sheet off Marlena's face. Raiden could already tell that she had been beaten up by the bruises on her face.

"What happened, Adam?"

"From the exam I took for your sister. I found it to be that she was beaten up before death, and her throat was sliced, killing her." While hearing this, Raiden cried in sorrow for losing his sister and the pain she went through. After a couple of minutes, Raiden could hold back the tears and catch his breath.

"From the body, I could subtract some latent prints."

"Any idea who?" Raiden asked.

"Nope, I would need to take it to Nova for it to be processed, and you know how they don't care about anything outside of their area."

"Yeah, right." Raiden agreed. He wished they would help, or the doctor could do it himself, but there were only a few places with electricity that the machines could run on. Even the doctor's office with solar panels on the roof could not create enough electricity. The doctor collaborated with basic people on bargain trades and did not make enough to afford to buy the electricity needed to run it.

In Sand Town, only a few places, like businesses and wealthy people, could afford solar panels. The city itself had windmills out of town to power its office and all the equipment used to run the town. It would share the power with its citizens, but only if they could pay, or if it saved the power in battery cells that filled the warehouse town for emergencies. The town also sold some power cells at the arsenal, and some to neighboring small towns, and to Nova.

Nova was the best sale, but it was the only place in the Shairyn Dynasty with full power. The cell power was used in Nova to charge weapons, other military equipment, and the government office if the power source went out. That never really happened, and no one knew where their electricity came from in Nova. So, they only bought power cells occasionally.

"Ready to identify the other body?" Adam asked.

"I guess." Replies Raiden.

Adam walked over to the second table.

"Again, are you ready, Raiden?"

"Just do it."

Again, Adam lifted the sheet, and under, as Raiden had predicted, was his nephew, Robert. This time, Raiden held back the emotions and asked, "How did he die?"

"It looks like he was defending the house. There is gunpowder in his hands. A sign that he fired a gun. And stab mark explaining he was stabbed in the right side to slowly bleed to death."

"fuck" Raiden whispered.

"It looks from the marks that the person was close to him and used a military-style knife. When the bodies were brought here, I noticed he was still in his night clothes, meaning this was done at night. Probably late at night, explaining why no one noticed until morning, when billows of smoke were in the town. From what the sheriff told me about the farm, all buildings were set on fire and had burned to the ground by the next afternoon."

Night? Raiden thought. What would a soldier or private be doing up late at night? Shouldn't he be with the other soldiers? They usually stayed in town and were under supervision the whole time they stayed, which was only two to three days. They arrived on schedule, the exact time every month. Making it so the businesses that collaborate with them on resources for Nova knew exactly when to have everything ready.

"Adam, why were the privates able to leave town? Aren't they under supervision the whole time they are in town?"

"You are correct, but they had to stay late for some local supplies, not being in town yet. The Major First Class of the group let the Privates have a night off to relax."

Now the question going through Raiden's mind was, where did they go? Was that where they learned about his address? It was good that Ariel and Diego did that part of the investigation. Raiden was sure whoever the leak was, he would almost kill them for telling the private that information.

"Thank you, Adam?"

"What do you want done now?" Adam asked.

"How about you set up a local wake and then burial in the local cemetery? I have the money to cover the cost of all of it." Raiden replies.

"Okay, I will start setting that up today. It should all be set up by tomorrow and scheduled for three days from now."

"Again, thanks." Raiden stuck his hand out and gave Adam a good handshake. Then, he went for the hall door, out into the lobby, waved at Beth, and was out and ready to find out what Ariel and Diego knew.

CHAPTER 21

Ariel and Diego walked over to the bar. Right in front was the local drunk Luke. He was normally inside, hammered already by 10 am, but this time he looked more awake and sober.

"Hey, how are you doing?" Ariel said.

"Stupid ass bartender kicked me out," Luke replies. Diego drank a little more than the rest of the crew and knew that had to suck. Back in the old days, that happened a lot to him, too.

"Why? What caused that?" Diego asked.

"Bartender says I was rude and almost punched him, so he kicked me out for a month. And now Jason will not let me buy my whiskey till the month is over, too." He said with a face of fury.

"That is too bad. We could help?" Diego points out.

"Would you?" Luke asked with a smile on his face.

"But we need to ask a question or two," Diego said.

"Okay," Luke replies.

"How long have you been sober?" Ariel asked.

"Over two weeks. And it royally sucks. My memory of the old days is coming back, and it is depressing." Diego remembered Luke talking when drunk about his past. Diego believed what Luke talked about was his enormous debt from gambling and not being able to pay. A dirty saloon owner was said to have killed his family in revenge. It was still rumored that the saloon owner was looking for Luke. But Luke's cousin had moved him out here quickly and told him to stay quiet and just survive. That is why the community thought that was the reason Luke was the local drunk idiot of Sand Town.

"We can help 100%," Diego said.

Luke shook his head excitedly.

"Okay, so do you know anything about soldiers being here in town?" Ariel asked.

"Yes, about a week ago," Luke replied.

"What did they do?" Diego asked.

"They were here for a monthly pickup."

"How long?" Ariel asked.

"I believe four days for some late supplies getting into town," Luke answers. Ariel and Diego looked at each other and nodded. I agree that this makes sense as to why the soldiers stayed longer. But they both knew that soldiers were usually in the barn on the edge of town, and that was it.

"Did they do anything besides stay at the barn like normal?" asked Diego.

Luke answers, "Yes, they did."

"Do you know why?"

"From what I know, it was because of supplies being late, but don't quote me." Ariel noticed Luke was giving off signs he was an intelligent person when he was not drunk.

Both Ariel and Diego figured the soldiers went to the bar that night.

"Anything happened that night?" Diego asked.

"Yes. No one shared any liquor with me." That was a sign to Ariel. Despite his intelligence, Luke was addicted to alcohol.

"Besides that, Luke," Ariel replied with a frown on her face.

"Oh well, some soldier and his friend came out buzzed. The guy who I believe was the leader of the group was angry because of the incident that happened that day."

"Was it the incident with Marlena?" Ariel asked.

"I believe so," Luke said. "They left the town a little later."

That was a good sign that it was the group that committed the crime. Especially with what they were complaining about and how they left town late at night.

"Do you have any idea how they found out about where she lived?" Ariel asked.

"Rumor is that it was the bartender, Frank. He skipped town immediately after Raiden's family was found dead."

That made sense. He was a shady guy and was always looking for more ways to make money no matter the circumstances, but now that he left town, how were they going to find him, verify the story, and get revenge?

"Thanks, Luke. We will go in and get you something to drink," Diego told Luke.

Ariel and Diego went to the door of the local bar, Namony's. It was a weird name to most people in the town, but it was special to the owner for some reason. The two walked in. Ariel noticed the bar was just the same as last night: dark, with the same old people at the bar counter, and just as last night, the same bartender stood.

They walked up to the bar and sat down. The bartender walked over, ready to talk about their order. Then realized it was Ariel from last night. Before asking for the orders, the Bartender asked Ariel what her name was.

Ariel replied, "Why are you asking?"

"I wanted to thank you personally for helping me with Raiden last night." The bartender says.

Ariel smiles. "That makes sense." She said with a grin on her face.

Diego looked at Ariel with a confused face.

"Raiden had gotten drunk, was rude to everyone here, and swung at me when I came to get him, so I knocked him out cold," Ariel said, looking at Diego. That made perfect sense to Diego - why Raiden had a headache this morning and the pain on the side of his face. The thought made Diego giggle and smile.

"He has always been like an ass at the bar when he gets drunk," Diego said.

"Again, thanks," the bartender said. "How may I help you?"

"First, what's your name?" Diego asked.

"Joe," the bartender responds.

"Okay, Joe, do you know anything about what happened here last week? The time when the Nova soldiers were here."

Joe was still thinking for a minute before he answered. "Frank and I had to work extra hours because the soldiers had a day off. The crowd was enormous, and I did not see too much, but I noticed one private. Confronted Frank, grabbed him, and threatened him. Frank was pretty shaken up for the rest of the night."

That made Diego and Ariel know money was not the cause of the information getting leaked. It was because he was frightened, but to them, that still was no excuse for letting the group know where the family lived.

"Do you have any Idea where he is now?" Diego asked.

"Rumor is that he left town and won't be coming back," Joe answered.

That made sense. Frank knew Raiden, so it was no surprise that he would leave after the results of telling the privates where Raiden's family lived. They knew what happened. They figured it was time to let Raiden know what they knew.

"Last question, and then we will take a full bottle of whiskey."

"Okay," the bartender replies.

"Do you know which building Frank lived in and if he took a horse or was traveling on foot?" Diego asked.

"It is said most of his stuff is still in the apartment. The landlord has yet to clean it. He is waiting for the Marshall to inspect it first. Frank bought one of the best-traveling horses he could afford, according to Richard, the horse trader. His stable is by the blacksmith shop." Joe said.

Joe went to the end of the bar to grab a substantial-sized bottle of whiskey and a small pair of shot glasses. He went back to Diego and Ariel and gave them the good-sized bottle. Ariel put five silver coins on the counter, which was more than needed. Joe handed over the bottle and then laid the two shot glasses down and poured the whiskey shots.

"On the house for helping me last night."

Diego and Ariel took the shots. Good aftertaste, both thought, especially Diego, thinking of the good old days. Ariel and Diego left the building. Waved at Luke. When Luke realized they had not lied to him. He had a huge smile on his face as Diego handed over the bottle of whiskey. Luke was so happy he just walked off, dazed with joy. The two then started off to the doctor's office to find Raiden.

CHAPTER 22

Raiden met with Diego and Ariel just a few buildings away from the saloon. Across the street, just a few buildings down, was Marshall's office. It was easy for the Marshall to see the group meet as he looked out the front office window. The Marshall's office was a small building in the middle of the block. Made of brick outside. Inside, it looked like a big open room when you first walked in, but after a few minutes, you could notice that the south wall was four jail cells. The cells were open to the public, with thick bars separating each cell, and a door on the north side of each cell. The three cells look small and mostly for one person, but the fourth was a bigger cell made for a group of people. The Marshall knew Raiden and his friends had been all across town, being nosy about the events of last week.

It was time for the Marshall to confront the group and make sure they understood that if they caused trouble, they would all be in the jail cells, the Marshall thought to himself. The Marshall was an outstanding officer and would do his best to enforce law and justice in the region, but he also knew that the crimes committed last week could not be investigated and no law could be enforced because of it all dealing with the Dynasty army. But the Marshall knew that would not matter to Raiden or his friends. They were going to stir up trouble. And this town did not need that happening.

The Marshall walked over to his fancy oak wooden desk, picking up his gun holster with a Glock 27, which was close to the front door of the building. Marshall put it in the handgun Holster and walked to the door. "Deputy, watch the office, I am warning Raiden." The Marshall said as he opened the door.

"Yes, sir," the Deputy answers, walking out of the small kitchen next to the front desk office. Marshall walked on the tarp street where the city was hiring workers to help move the sticky tarp. It was not understood why the streets of this town had a black tarp on it and other parts were gravel and some were the ancient material called cement. Cement was everywhere around, but was crumbling apart. No one knew how to repair it or even really knew what it was made of, besides sometimes having metal bars in the middle of it. Poor people living in the town broke the cement up to get to the bars and sell it back in the arsenal.

There was a crew of young men up the street digging up the tarp and putting it into a semi tipping trailer as the Marshall walked across the street towards Raiden and his friends.

"RAIDEN!" the Marshall shouted out as he crossed the street. It started the group, and the Marshall could tell from the faces they made that they were not happy that it was he who shouted it out as he walked up to the group.

"First off, I am sorry for what happened to your family, Raiden."

"Thanks, Marshall," Raiden replies. Raiden knew that was just a show to the public, so they thought he was a gentleman, but Raiden knew that was not why he was confronting them.

"But I have heard from around town you are stirring up some trouble?" the Marshall pointed out.

"I do not know what you are talking about, Marshall. We just got back in town." Raiden replied to the Marshall.

"Is that so?" the Marshall said with a light laugh.

"Yeah, 100%, sir," Ariel said.

"Well, just to let you know, I am investigating the murders of your family and finding your daughter. So, do not get in my way, Raiden. You need to rest and recover from all this." The Marshall said with irritation. Raiden and the crew knew it was all bullshit. If you were not a dumdass, you would already know that the Marshall would not do or could do nothing because it involved the Dynasty Army, and since Raiden's daughter was out of the region, the Marshall could not do anything.

"Whatever you say, Marshall," Raider replies.

"One question, Marshall?" Diego asked as the Marshall was turning around to go back to the office.

"What do you know about all of this? Any Idea who the murderer might be?"

"Sorry, Diego, but this is an ongoing investigation. I will let you know once I solve it and the guilty person is in the jail cell." Again, the crew knew that was a lie. The Marshall would not do anything from this point on.

The Marshall turned around and headed back to the office, waving at a few citizens down the street as he crossed the street and back into his office. Raiden, Diego, and Ariel all knew it was time to get out of town.

CHAPTER 23

Raiden and his friends arrived back at Diego's around noon. The kids were playing outside, and Diego's wife, Sarah, was hanging clothes on the clothesline out back to dry for the day. Diego waved at Sarah. She saw it, smiled, and blew Diego a kiss across the yard. Raiden, Ariel, and Diego got off the horses and walked them to the barn. The fence connected to the barn covered about five acres of prairie that Diego got ownership of from his grandfather before he passed away. They took the saddles off each horse and then walked the horses over to the gate, opening it, and releasing all three of the horses to go relax on the prairie for the rest of the day.

The kids saw Diego walking towards the house, and they ran over to him, gave him a big hug, and started talking about all the fun and new things they had done this morning. Sarah put the last shirt on the clothesline and walked over to Diego to give him a wonderful kiss and hug. Ariel walked inside the house, going to rest for a little.

Raiden stood next to the fence and stared out into the prairie, watching the horses wander off and eat grass in the field. It was a peaceful view and a straightforward way for Raiden to relax his mind. But he couldn't. It was racing around as he tried to think of what to do next. He knew he couldn't just stand around. He was torn between his rage because of the murders and his need to find his niece. But he had no clue what to do first. Both were going to take time. The private was back in Nova, most likely. He couldn't be touched for now, and the crew that kidnapped his niece could be about anywhere since they traveled on the mud river. The question now was how to do it. Raiden stood there thinking of ways to reach both goals. He did not realize that it had been five hours since the crew and he had gotten back to Diego's farm. He had decided on what had to be done. He had to leave and get more information on the kidnappers and if he stirred up trouble on his way to find his niece, so he felt. He was finding his family; he thought to himself.

Raiden stood up straight and walked over to the house. He saw Diego's family cleaning up after dinner and Ariel drinking beer on the front porch. As he walked towards the porch door, he made eye contact with Diego and Ariel to signal he was going out back and wanted them to join him.

It took Diego a little bit before he was done helping his family clean up, and for Ariel to finish her drink. Once they both walked onto the back porch, it was time for Raiden to let them know what he was doing.

"Okay, I want to let you both know I love you and that you are my best friends. But I can't stay here. I need to find Jennifer, and I must find out who the private soldier is. I am leaving in the morning."

They both nodded their heads and agreed with Raiden. Raiden looked a little confused at first, like he was waiting for a response, but more verbal, not just a head nod. Ariel noticed he was having difficulty with their response and asked, "What time in the morning?"

Despite his puzzlement, Raiden answers, "Sunrise. I need to get stuff from the farm before I leave tomorrow."

"I already stopped at the farm for you. There is a bag inside under the spare bed with the back of what was left of your belongings, specifically the stash you had under the kitchen floor," Diego said.

The Face that Raiden made explained well that he was not expecting that.

"How did you know?' he asked.

"Robert told me about finding a treasure a long time ago. I assumed it was yours."

This was a relief to Raiden. It meant he didn't need to go to the farm. Hearing that his family had been killed was hard, but seeing where his family had been killed would only add more to the devastation he was dealing with. Right now, he had to save Jessica.

"Do we leave at sunrise, then still?" Ariel asked.

"We? I am going on this quest myself, and neither of you needs to go."

"Jennifer is my niece!" Diego and Ariel said at the same time. That was true, Raiden thought. Ariel was the sister of Jennifer and Robert. Making her their aunt, and Diego was like family, making him the other uncle. "We want her safe, and we want to make sure that Private never gets a chance at doing anything like this again to anyone," Ariel said.

"So, you want to do this with me?"

"You'd better believe it!" Diego said, and Ariel shook her head, agreeing with Diego.

"What about your Family, Diego?'

"They're good. My wife knows me too well," Diego said with a smile on his face. Diego had already talked to his wife about helping Raiden however he could, and she was supportive of it, no matter what it took.

"Okay then, we take off tomorrow at dawn and save my niece," Raiden said, with a look of energy and determination.

CHAPTER 24

Present

Even after a magnificent effort to drive the Shairyn Knights back to save the people of the village, it wasn't looking good. The knights were still winning. Ariel had a severe injury now, not just the arm injury she had at first, making this all on Diego and Raiden.	They both ducked behind a rubble wall, half its original height. The city the villagers lived in was turning into nothing, just crumbles of what it once was. Raiden and Diego felt guilty.

"I am out of bullets," Raiden said. Diego nodded, pointing out he was out too, but as Raiden and Diego prepared to be defeated. Raiden saw a rocket from the roof of a building down the street fly by them and hit the building where some of the Knights were. The building exploded, with a ball of flames devouring the building. Turning it into ashes and crumbles of what it once was.

Immediately down the street where the rocket came from, Diego and Raiden heard someone say Fire. Spontaneously, automatic assault weapons fired off. They saw some of the leading Knights giving instructions to fall back. Knights shot off their plasma weapons to cover while the rest retreated out of sight, hitting some of the mystery soldiers, but right after, the Knights started falling to the ground. Raiden believed a sniper was shooting out of sight at one of the neighboring buildings. Raiden looked around the wall to get more details of the battle.

The building where the Knights were before, while hunting Diego and Raiden, was torn down, with walls that had fallen on the knights. Some knights lay in the debris of the fallen building on the ground. He could see knights a block down the street preparing to get the plasma weapons that the other knights had before being shot dead. As the commander of the knights gave orders to the knights to shoot their plasma weapons to cover two other knights who ran up to get the weapons from the fallen knights, Another Rocket took off down the street. The knights with the plasma weapons ducked behind the debris. But the rocket flew right past them and hit where the commander and the other knights were gathered. Some knights took off from the place of command but were shot down by the snipers. Once the rocket hit and exploded, knights were thrown across the street from the explosion and landed on the broken cement roads. The knight in charge of the group vanished into the flames of the explosion.

Just as the last handful of knights vanished into another building down the street to figure out what to do, automatic weapons started shooting from the same building. Right after, two of the mystery soldiers came out of the building, flagging whoever was in command down the street that all the knights had been taken care of.

Raiden and Diego were wondering what this group was going to do to them. Just as they were preparing to run, the group commander shouted out, "Archangels, we are here in peace." Raiden was not comfortable with that name. It referred to the leading angels in the war against the evil god-like character called the devil, according to some of the elderly. It was said to have come from the forbidden book. Raiden did not believe they were that important. The Dynasty had spread the word that they were demons out to cause chaos and nothing else. But the public disagreed, calling them Archangels.

"Is that so? "Raiden replies.

"Yes, it is… Raiden." The commander said. Raiden was worried. The commander knew his name, meaning there was a chance the Dynasty knew too, which put Diego's family at risk.

"I know you are out of ammo, so please step out and talk." Said the commander.

Raiden and Diego thought they were going to die because of the Knights a minute ago, so it wouldn't make much of a difference if they died because of this crew that won this battle. Both stood up from behind the rubble, prepared to surrender. But the minute they stood up, they heard a soldier say, "It is the Archangels!" The crowd of soldiers started chanting, "Angels! Angels! Angels!" The commander raised his hand to signal the soldiers to quiet down. All of them had smiles on their faces.

The commander walked over to Raiden and stuck his hand out for a handshake. Raiden followed and gave the commander a handshake.

People across the land are talking about you guys as heroes. Neither Raiden nor Diego knew that.

"My Name is Russell, but as you can tell, my crew calls me the commander." Now it was obvious to Raiden that they were safe for the moment. He shouted out to Ariel and a crowd of villagers, "It is safe, you can all come out!" Ariel and the group of villagers walked out of the building behind Raiden and Deigo with worried faces. But as they came out looking and noticed that dead knights were lying across the ground, while Raiden and Deigo stood firmly talking to the Commander, the villagers started crying in joy.

A few women and children ran up to Raiden to hug him and said, Thank you. Ariel walked out with some kids around her with a smile on her face. Diego walked over to Ariel to check her arm and shoulder. "I am good," she said.

"You must be Ariel," Russell said, sticking his hand out again. Ariel shook it, but with a puzzled face. She looked at Raiden and Diego showing.

"We are Soldiers of Gateway," Russell said.

Even with the help that Russell and his crew gave them, Raiden already knew that Gateway was no gratuitous community. Because of the help, the clan would say that Raiden and the crew were in debt now, and someday they would need to repay that debt. But it was true Raiden owed them for saving the lives of Diego Ariel, the villagers, and himself. As a result of the battle, it was not unlikely that the villagers could live in the town anymore, as Raiden was thinking of what to do with the villagers now. Russell walked over to Raiden to confront him with an idea of helping with this situation.

"Angels? I have a wonderful idea that can help these villagers." Russell said.

Raiden looked up and thought, oh shit, what now? Before he could reply to Russell. Russell let out his idea.

"There is a town outside of our city with plenty of open houses that these people could use. And because of the Celtic Clans, the Sharyn Army would never confront it."

Raiden knew that was true, especially after this battle. Even being upset and wanting revenge, going straight to battle with the Celtic Clans would be a mistake for the Dynasty.

Rumors were that a war was ready to start between the Dynasty and the Union, making a conflict with the Clans unwise. It was obvious, even with the Leader and council of the town still talking, they would eventually come to an agreement for the Clan's protection.

Right after, the council agreed to move to the land of the clan. Russel and his crew brought in a herd of horses and multiple wagons. It only took a few hours, and the families and people of the town were on their way to the clan's city. The dynasty called it the Unholy City to keep people away from it and not do any trading with it, but a normal person in the Flatlands, or even in the arsenal, knew better. They all know the real name, Gateway.

CHAPTER 25

The people and the army reached the small towns around Gateway a few days later, before sunset for the day. The small towns welcomed them. Small groups of warriors were guarding the entry into the towns. It was full of small homes and businesses. Only a handful of blocks away from the walls of Gateway. As they came closer to Gateway, they noticed how the city looked like what people thought Nova was like. Thick Cement walls surround the city to protect it from invasion. Raiden, like most in the flatlands, thought that people couldn't use cement and didn't know how. It was mostly wasted material across the flatlands. As the group entered the city, Raiden looked around, seeing the same towers he saw on the runes of the windy city, but here they were lit up. Some you could still see how time had affected them, but most stood tall with lights behind glass windows. To Raiden, it was amazing to see a place similar to the ruins he hunted in, alive and well. The towers stood taller than the eye could see. Before fully reaching the location of the giant towers, there were smaller, multiple-floor buildings. A handful of lights on every block of the street. Raiden could easily tell because of the street lights at every corner and the light on in every house and building that this city had electricity.

People walked across the streets of the city wearing different clothes that Raiden, Diego, and Ariel had never seen. It was in bright dye colors of green, pink, purple, orange, and neon shades. Colors that most people of the flatlands had never seen, and that were said to only be in Nova. Houses had signs on the Front wall with symbols of some kind. Some were the same, and others were different.

You could tell the signs had many languages and cultures related to the design of the sign. This interested Raiden, as it revealed a society composed of many clans and cultures, not just the Irish and Scottish. This helped Raiden understand more that it was nothing like the Dynasty said it was, calling it the Unholy City. My ass this city is unholy, Raiden thought.

There were businesses everywhere, from ones on the ground floor of the buildings to food carts on the sidewalk. The smell of the food was amazing. Raiden saw many stores, not just a general store like in Sand Town. In the stores and on the carts of Gateway, there were sales on items and food that Raiden had never heard of.

The most intriguing thing he saw was a store selling hundreds of unique books. Finding literature in the flatlands and even at the arsenal was rare, but here there were so many choices. Diego had to pull on Raiden's shirt to get him out of the blur and back in line with the group they were walking with in town.

The group arrived at the giant community center. Members of the clans opened the doors and helped them get their stuff in and settle in the center.

Russel told the villagers that the next day, the village council could talk to the clan leaders about setting up an agreement and moving their stuff into one of the small towns around Gateway called Maplewood. Raiden, Diego, and Ariel found a spot in the community center and were preparing to put their blankets down and get ready to rest for the night. Russel showed up just as they finished.

"What are you doing?" he asked.

"Settling down for the night," Raiden replies.

"That is Rubbish. You are the Archangels. The leaders of the Clans can't wait to see you," Russel said with a smile., "We have plenty of things to talk about."

Raiden looked at the other two and could tell this was not what they wanted, but that they all knew it was a requirement. Russel walked them out of the hall and a few blocks. As they walked down the blocks, they entered the area where the towers stood. Metal and glass composed some towers; others consisted only of glass. Around the towers, it was darker, with shade between the buildings. But there were more street lights that lit up the area.

The tower that Russell was taking them to, one of the city's tallest towers, had reflective glass covering it. The tower stood in a more open area. There was a metal fence around the building.

Two soldiers stood in front of the gate to pass through the metal fence. It was amazing, Raiden, how much metal was in the city. In the Flatlands and the Dynasty, metal was rare. In their lands, there were no mines or ways to get metal besides finding it and selling it at the arsenal. They walked up to the doorway to pass the fence. Two soldiers stood by the door. From the uniforms and symbols on their armor, it was easy to tell they were not just soldiers, but warriors.

Once inside the building, they entered a huge open lobby with stairs at the end. More warriors stood guarding the pathway to the stairs. The stairs were two stories up, and at the top, on the right and left, were more stairs to the upper floors. Right in front was a big, thick wooden door with a symbol made of what was thought to be an extremely rare metal called steel. It must have been the symbol of the entire clan, not just the symbol of the separate groups of the clan that Raided saw all around the city.

The warriors stood guard and opened the doors once Russell said a code in a foreign language. The room they entered was a wide-open room with a round table in the middle, with the leaders of the clans sitting around the round table. On the side in front of Raiden were four open seats. Russel took one and waved at Raiden, Diego, and Ariel to sit next to him.

Once they all sat down and the warriors shut the doors behind them, they saw a large group of leaders. Men and women were dressed in many outfits. Some in business suits that were said to be all over Nova, to ancient-looking warrior suits, and then some dressed in robes with images of knights, dragons, stars, and many symbols of the other cultures in Gateway.

The leader of the clans stood up. "Welcome to Gateway. My name is Mangus, leader of all clans and master of the thunder clan," he said in an upper voice while raising his wooden pint. Raiden was sure it was full of ale. Still sitting, the rest of the clan leaders did the same. Then, taking a big drink of the ale, they all slammed their pints on the table with smiles across their faces.

Raiden replies, "Thank you."

The leader sat back down and put his elbows on the table with his hands together in a calm, fist-looking style. "Now let's talk," Mangus said. Raiden and his friends all knobbed yes.

"You, the archangels, have been causing some great chaos for the Dynasty, we hear?"

Raiden replies, "I guess we have."

"Good," Mangus said. "But it looks like you guys need help of some sort."

"You might say that," Raiden answered.

"Yes, we do," Mangus replied with a small laugh. "We can supply you with better weapons and armor to fight the Dynasty, but at a price."

"You can, can you? What weapons and armory are you talking about and at what price?" Raiden asked.

"Good question." Mangus replied, "We have bulletproof armory and plasma blast-resistant shielding and ..." Mangus tried to continue, but before Mangus could finish, a clan leader with a symbol on his outfit, looking like what in the old tales was called a lion, stood up. "This is outrageous! We do not even know." He shouted, but the leader interrupted him before he could fully object.

Mangus shouts, while slamming his fist to the table, "Sit down! They are fighting the dynasty, too." The clan leader sat back down with a frustrated look on his face.

"Sorry for the interruption," Mangus said. "Besides the shields and armor, we also have some weapons that will come in handy against the dynasty defense forces. Which will be the next group of soldiers you will fight, I can bet." Raiden understood that. After the knights were defeated, the dynasty was going to up the game soon with a goal of revenge.

Raiden knew there was a catch to all of this, but really didn't know what it would be.

"What is the cost of all this help you are willing to provide us with?"

"Wonderful Question. We want you to help us get a load of supplies heading to Nova."

To Raiden, that was weird to ask. Obviously, they could fight the dynasty with no problem. To him, it was shady that they asked him and his group to do this, but they were in debt to the clan now.

"We can see about helping, but why do you need our help?"

It was easy to see that the question was not the correct answer. Mangus slammed his fist on the table. "How dare you even ask? It is none of your business. You owe us and are lucky we offer these goods, and that is all you need to know."

"Yes, you are correct. It is none of my business." Raiden answered.

"Good, that you understand that," Mangus replies. "The mission will happen in three days. You will need to take off tomorrow. Is that understood?"

Raiden, Deigo, and Ariel all nobbed yes.

"You will be armed properly for the mission and will be given your full equipment once you return." Mangus waved at them to leave. "Go get the equipment for tomorrow and be ready to take off at dawn.", Mangus said, and the Guards opened the door. The group walked out of the room. Before the doors were closed, they could hear a big argument breaking out in the room. Some of the clan leaders were not in favor of them getting the supplies they were getting. It sounded like some didn't trust them to do the mission at all.

The warrior guards at the bottom of the stairs led them out of the building and passed through the gate. A Warrior stood at the gate and led them to a Warehouse-type building. Inside were multiple warriors picking up supplies from the endless number of tables with choices of weapons Raiden and the crew had never seen or heard of. The first table Raiden checked was swords and axes, but they were different. You could tell by each that they were super sharp, but you could see blue lines on the outside close to the edge of the blades. That is when Raider saw a warrior take one sword and walk over to a Dynasty soldier-looking figure, along with a big metal plate standing up next to it. The warrior swung the sword, slicing right through the armor of the soldier figure. After that, the warrior walked in front of the sheet of Metal. The warrior somehow turned on the blue strips and swung again. The blue strips must have been heating or something, Raiden thought, because it sliced through the metal like a knife through butter. Raiden got one sword and a scabbard to hold it in. Before leaving the table, he saw a dagger, looking like the sword he had. He knew Ariel could use them.

Ariel looked around and saw bows, arrows, and quivers, but now with a million more types than she had ever seen before. She saw a warrior shoot multiple arrows. One looked like it was poison, one like it froze whatever it hit, and one like the one she used in the battle that exploded. The Bows were different. One had something that made a red dot land wherever the arrow was going to hit. The arrow penetrated through the armor the figure was wearing. The armor she was wearing was nothing she had seen before. That was the armor that the Dynasty Defense Force wore in battle. Ariel felt she would need something like that for future battles.

She grabbed a large quiver that would fit around thirty arrows. It fit well over her shoulders, then she loaded it up with ten explosive arrows, ten freezing ones, another five poison arrows, and five more armor-penetrating arrows. She now had to pick the proper Bow for all of this. At the next table, she found the choices of Bows. Some basic bows are made of metal instead of wood with a strong, firm bowstring. It felt like no weather would stop the bowstring from working. The last bow she saw was complex. It was a red dot for close range, but it also had a scope.

She took it to the doorway to the warehouse and looked through it. She could see almost four blocks down the street, and at the end of the four blocks, on the wall of a house, was the red dot. Her amazement was profound; could this really shoot an arrow that far? She went back to the table, and a man stood on the other side of the table now. It must have been the merchant of the sales. "What's your name?" she asked. The merchant turned around to see who was talking. He was an extremely bizarre white skin man. With the top of his head bald, and around it a thick amount of brownish hair.

"You can call me Walter, ma'am." She nodded her head in agreement.

"So, Walter, will this bow shoot an arrow over 1200 yards away?"

"Can I look at what bow you have?" Walter asked. Ariel handed over the bow, and Walter looked at it for a few minutes, and then pointed at the number and name of Maxell.

"You can 100% shoot the arrow that far. It is a Maxwell 300, the best bow for long and short-distance shots."

"Is there a certain arrow that works with this?"

"About any arrow works with it and can go that distance, but the best I would use is a Maxwell long shot." Ariel took it, walked back to the quivers, grabbed two more, and then grabbed sixty of the Maxwell 300 long shots. She would carry the special arrows, and the horse she rode could carry the other two quivers with most of the Maxwell 300s.

She handed over five of the explosive arrows and said, "Thank you," with a huge smile on her face. She could not wait to see what she could do with this equipment.

At the end of the row of tables, Diego was going through dozens of choices of guns and explosives. He found the Glock G23 that Raider shot, along with multiple clips and packs of bullets to add to the clips. Raider was going to be happy. But what Diego was happy about was that he found multiple automatic assault rifles he liked, along with long-distance sniper rifles and a sizable number of explosives, which he loves.

He grabbed two M27 IAR, and he filled his duffle bag half full of the 5.56mm bullets for the guns. Then grabbed two more Glock G23 and five magazines for each one for him and Ariel to use.

He then walked over to the explosives and looked to see what they had. One was a mine he had never seen before, for what the package showed. It looked like it was a magnetic gadget. It would be good off from remote with half-mile ratios. The thing would cause a magnetic wave to cover a ¼ mile radius, messing up any kind of technology that was being used within that radius. Diego thought they would help when they were the ones attacking, but it would be great for defense when they went against the next group of Knights or against the Defense Force that Ariel was always talking about. He saw a few more interesting traps. One would set off a magnetic force again, but this time it was to attract all metal objects towards it from 25-yard distances. Then came his basic favorite hand grenades, which were the basic pin and handle. There was also a bag to hold around five hand grenades. Diego was not sure what the clan thought was better than this, but he would have to see.

Once all three found what they thought was best, they met outside. Raiden could tell that Ariel and Diego were happy with what they found. Raiden handed over the special dagger to Ariel, who smiled even more, and Deigo handed over the Glock G23 to Raiden and Ariel, along with the five magazines he got for each of them. They all three started back towards the community center to get some rest. The next couple of days were going to be serious, and they would need their energy for it.

CHAPTER 26

It had been over a year since Jennifer had seen any family. She still couldn't believe how the night of the attack was her last night of freedom. She was being used as a slave for physical labor and to cook for the crew of the tradesmen. One man tried to rape her, but before he achieved anything, he was neutered by Jennifer with a cooking knife she would use later that day to cook for the crew. The rest of the crew thought it was funny and justified. That man was kicked off the boat while on the river. No one was sure if he made it to the shore or if he drowned in the rapids of the mud river.

These men were shady, as her uncle always said, but they had a code of honor. No stealing from the crew, just stealing from other people, no violence between members of the crew, never harming women, especially sexually. Forced slavery was ok and an eye for an eye when it came to the public towards them.

Jennifer had run towards the Love Blood River, the elderly from Sand Town called it the Wapsipinicon, but no one knew much about where that name came from. After the soldiers murdered her family, she fainted in the field just a little north of the river. The men of the trade group saved her from the local wolves, but she was told afterward that she owed them. They said she would work for them as a cook and labor slave until she earned her freedom back. Jennifer was still clueless about how to earn her freedom back.

The boat the tradesmen used was an old steam-run tugboat. In most places, solar or wind-generated power was used for the engines of the boats, but these were coal-run engines. Authorities forbade them on most land, but not on the rivers, especially the mud river. They moved a small barge with material to trade once they got to the city, The Big Easy. They had traded crops with the Clan a couple of weeks ago when they were close to the city. They would trade some other material to upgrade the engine of the tugboat to be cheaper to run. Coal was getting expensive, and it was heavy, meaning that with all the coal on the boat, it would move more slowly, costing them more money.

Jennifer walked onto the deck of the boat after finishing lunch, ready to shout out to the crew that lunch was ready. They needed to anchor the boat and get some food while they could. Before she told them, she looked around and for the last 34 days she was in a part of the North continent she had never known of. Seeing it was hot once they passed Gateway, it was easy to tell where the desert started, even from the boat, but the more they got to the gulf, the more it was what the crew called tropical. Diverse kinds of trees grow on the banks of the river. They were called palm trees. People said the trees had never grown this far up the muddy river before the Final War. People across the South talked about how the world was vastly different before then. Some even told tales of the North Continent being called the USA and being the superpower nation of the world.

The crew had more tales and stories to tell about the world before the Final War than anyone up in the land of the Shairyn Dynasty. While at the dock at Gateway, she even heard of a place called the Union. She had never heard of any other nation besides the Dynasty.

She shouted out, and the crew heard immediately. The anchor went down, and five crew members and the captain came up the stairs. Once they were all down at the table, Jennifer came down to serve the food. She was good at taking supplies they got from villages along the river and making some of the best food the men could ever dream of. Her mom always said she would be a skilled chef someday. Nowadays, she knew her mom wasn't lying when she said that.

After lunch, all the men of the crew had big smiles on their faces.

"Wonderful food today." The captain pointed out. The other men of the crew all nodded yes in agreement.

"You're welcome," Jennifer replies. The captain signaled the crew to get back to work. They all frowned for a second but knew in a few more days they could have a vacation for a week or more while at THE BIG EASY. The crew went up the stairs to get back to work. Before the captain got up to return upstairs, Jennifer asked, "Captain?"

"Yes." The captain replied.

"You told me a while ago that I needed to earn to not be a slave. What do I need to earn?"

It was easy to tell from the captain's face that this was not a question he wanted to answer today. But with respect, he still replied in a calm voice. "Jennifer, from all you have done on this trip with feeding the crew and the hard work to maintain the cleanliness of this tugboat, I was going to offer you a deal."

A deal, thought Jennifer. What kind of deal is he talking about? "What is that?" Jennifer asked.

"I was going to offer you a job. Same thing now, just you get paid, and it is just a contract on how long you stay here on the tugboat."

This blew Jennifer's mind. Employment and money. Jennifer wanted to get back up to her hometown, but she knew it was dangerous for her to do that herself, and down here, the crew was the only people she knew. She had already heard from the people of Gateway that a group called The Archangels was stirring up trouble with the Dynasty, and she had bet that it was her uncles and Aunt. Of course, she wasn't sure. It was the perfect deal, she thought, a ride back to Flatland Trade Center and get paid in the process.

"How much did she ask?'

"Well, depending on how much we make and how much it costs for the upgrade, it should be around 50 in gold coins and 25 in silver coins." That put a big smile on Jennifer's face. That would be plenty, she thought, and with her just being a cook and staff, it would be worth it 100%. She could see her fiancé again.

"If I can get off when we get back to the arsenal, it's a Deal," she said. She stuck her hand out for a shake. She learned that it was a sign of respect for an agreement in one of the little towns where she got some food supplies. The captain took her hand and shook it. 'I will also give you some extra for working now till we get to the dock at THE BIG EASY." The captain turned around and walked up the stairs, yelling that she agreed. The crew cheered in happiness that they got to keep the excellent cook. Jennifer just smiled; she was going to be home soon and have plenty of money once this was all over.

CHAPTER 27

The rumor through the army was that the First squad of Shairyn Knights had failed against the group of Bandits. To the Emperor of the Shairyn Dynasty, that wasn't good. The generals who sat in front of him could tell he was furious because of the failure of the knights. They couldn't believe a squad of knights failed to defeat a group of Bandits.

"What happened?!!!! How did a small group of bandits defeat a squad of Knights?!!!" The emperor asked while slamming his hands on the table in front of him. The Generals sitting at the table all knew this would not end well. It was still a mystery to them what had happened. One of Lieutenant Jefferson's squads found a person from that village who was easily persuaded by money. They had left the group after the event because the clans were helping the bandits. The clans wanted the individual for stealing from a merchant in Gateway.

"Emperor, we know little, but one of my squads found a man with information." Said Lieutenant Jefferson.

"What Information?"

"From my understanding, sir, the man says it was the Celtic Clans Army that helped the bandits survive." The emperor looked a little more at ease now, knowing that it had taken an army to defeat his squad of Shairyn Knights. The generals all looked at each other, surprised that Lieutenant Jefferson knew this, and they didn't. Jefferson signaled the Doorway guards to open the door. Once opened, three soldiers walked in with a young peasant. The peasant was wearing basic clothes. Jeans, T-shirt, and leather boots. It was easy to tell that he had been cleaned up. His medium-long hair was a shiny blond color now, not the dirt brown it was earlier. Once the four walked in, the door was closed.

Jefferson showed the peasant to a seat at the table. To the peasant, it was obvious that the old man at the end of the table was the emperor, and the men around the table were the military staff. The emperor looked older than the peasant had thought. He was an older man with thick gray and white hair. From just a look at the emperor's face, the peasant could see the scars from the battles the emperor had fought in the shadow war that made the Dynasty a superpower.

The dynasty had been around for the last couple of centuries or more, but it wasn't an empire until the Dynasty had won against the group of small kingdoms called the Legions. The legions spread across the west and south of the Dynasty. The Dynasty covered most of the northern part of the North Continent. With the legion south and west of it, covering most of the Flatlands until you get to the mountains. There were only a few ways to pass the mountains, and the Dynasty had yet to get to what travelers called the Golden

Coast, without costly conflict because of the weather or the mountains themselves.

The peasant was a little nervous, but from what Jefferson had told him, it would be worth it. So much gold, he thought. The Dynasty was rich, making it so that paying him the reward wouldn't hurt them at all.

"What's your name?" the emperor asked in a calm voice.

"They call me Alpha."

"Alpha, you say." the emperor replies.

"Yes, Your Highness." The emperor waved his hand at the three soldiers to leave. He then turned back to Alpha. "So, you know the truth of the event."

"Yes, I do you."

"Then please tell." The emperor commanded.

"Yes, sir. The town I was staying in was Crossroad. You know why the Knights were there, but it came out where the Archangels were defeated."

"WHAT! Did you call them?" the emperor asked, with flames of anger in his eyes.

"Sorry, sir." The thought that these scums were called archangels infuriated the emperor, but he needed to know more. "Continue," the emperor said.

"It was only three people," the peasant continued. "One person was wounded, and the other two ran out of ammunition; however, the Gateway Clan's army suddenly appeared." With Rockets and automatic weapons. They removed the knights and gathered the weapons. The emperor looked at some generals with a frown on his face. Now the Clan had more advanced weapons. With a little time, they could have the outline and make their copies soon. That wouldn't help with the war against the Union since the Clan and Union were allies. The Clan would at least sell armory supplies to the Union. The Generals were already thinking of ways to respond to the emperor once this peasant had left.

"Did you learn anything about the bandits that I should know?" the emperor asked. It was to tell Alpha that he was taking too long to tell the story.

"It is just three people. Two men and one woman. People say they are from around the Flatland Trade Center." This was a catch to the emperor; he had remembered there being an incident that happened in a town by the Trade Center that caused a problem with its people. That incident might have been what caused the bandits to campaign against the Dynasty.

"The Archangels asked about a Private, nicknamed Lucifer, and a young girl called Jennifer. They never really explained why, just that is who they were looking for." That rang the bell. That was the nickname of the private Jefferson, who was now the lieutenant who brought the witness..

"Is there anything else you can think of?"

"Not at this moment, your Highness." The emperor looked over at the guards by the door. They opened the doors. Outside in the hall stood the three soldiers.

"The soldiers will show you the way to where you can receive your reward for this information." Alpha turned around and walked to the door behind him. The emperor pointed and shook his hand at the soldiers outside in the hallway. They understood they should take the peasant to the bounty hunters. It was an agreement that they would take him to one of the emperor's allies up by the

North Pole, where he was wanted for fraud, robbery, and treason of the Frozen Kingdom.

As the door was closing, it was easy for the emperor to see the peasant try to run away once he saw the bounty hunters walking down the hall, with the soldiers stopping the peasant. The Frozen Kingdom would owe him for finding the financial terrorist who had stolen more than half of the king of the Frozen Kingdom's treasure.

"Lucifer!" the emperor shouted. "Is this all your fault?" The sudden accusation surprised Lucifer. He thought in frustration about how this could be his fault. He already had the responsibility of taking care of the mission against Gateway. Fighting the Bandits was a waste of time and shouldn't be his responsibility, Lucifer felt.

"Now, how do you stop these bandits from causing us more trouble?" The emperor asked, hoping to get a suitable answer from Lucifer and the generals. These bandits needed to be stopped now before they caused too much trouble. If Lucifer couldn't stop them, this was going to be his last mistake, with painful consequences.

The emperor felt it was time for him and the generals to pay attention to setting up the fight with the Union.

CHAPTER 28

Diego was on top of the hills on a beautiful prairie with green grass, natural flowers, and life all around, but sadly, he did not have time to absorb the healthy environment and happy feeling of life on the prairie. From the scope of the long-distance sniper rifle Diego had picked, he could see the train moving at a faster-than-normal speed down the tracks.

Like what clan warriors had talked about the night before, this wasn't just any train. Diego saw the strong roaring engine in the front with an armory car behind, then a special-looking car, which was the whole reason that the clan wanted this train and then another armed car after that, then just cars for metal, grains, refrigerated foods and a few cars set for basic supplies like recharged batteries, canned food and material for clothing,

It still bothered Diego thinking of how many people lived in areas like Sand Town that had people starving or begging for water, but the Dynasty didn't care. He could also see the crew waiting on the prairie for the train to come around the curve. Diego could see it in the straight part of the tracks a few miles before the curve.

Over the mic, something that Diego had never used before. "It is three miles counting. You Ready?" Diego said.

The leader of the crew responded to Diego, "Ready. Let's get started."

That was the key to begin. Diego looked through the scope and adjusted it for a more precise view of the train. On top of the train were a few soldiers watching out for attacks on the train, and a few others on the roof at the end of the train doing the same. He could also see the open holes where soldiers with automatic machine guns were ready to easily take out any group of thieves coming to rob the train.

Through the rifle, Diego could see a few faces through the openings that the men inside used to aim the machine guns. Diego took his time and adjusted to the light breeze going around. With the silencer on the rifle, not one soldier knew about the shots until one soldier fell backward with blood splattering on other soldiers from the back of his head. The other two soldiers in the machine gun cabinet of the train fell too, with a simpler pattern of falling to the floor of the cabinet. Diego liked how this was a sniper rifle and a reload-chambered gun. He had another thirteen bullets before reloading. He readjusted his aim and did the same scenario with the machine gun car next to the train engine. Same pace, same result. "Machine gun out," Diego said over the mic. Signaling the other group of warriors to head to the tracks.

Diego readjusted the scope, aiming at the front of the train by the engine. Diego could tell the engine part of the train was set up so a sniper or soldier from the outside of the train couldn't penetrate the walls, but all the soldiers on top were open targets.

Diego, taking his time, readjusted the scope to focus on the isolated soldiers. Their backs were turned to the others. One by one, he took out the soldiers with bullets straight to the back of their heads. The soldiers fell forward and off the train with no sound or notice from their fellow soldiers. Once the few on top that Diego could take out without notice, he aimed at the other soldiers, who were together. This felt like it was taking hours to do for Diego, but it was only taking a few minutes to do.

One of the new targets turned around to check on his fellow soldiers and immediately noticed that they were all missing. That was the key for Diego to take the next couple of shots. He was down to seven bullets in the chamber. As the other soldiers ran to see where their fellow soldiers were, Diego took them out. As the first two fell onto the roof of the car they were in, it was easy with Diego to get down to five shots. Once the two soldiers fell, an alarm went off across the train, with metal sheets sliding up on all cars with soldiers on them, and the soldiers ducked behind them to catch a second of breath and try to figure out what was happening. But with Diego on top of the hill, he had a good angle to still see the tops of the heads of some soldiers. He adjusted his aim and then used his last five bullets, taking out a few more soldiers and two snipers looking for him. "Reloading. Ariel, your turn," Diego said. Immediately after talking, dirt blasted up about two feet away from where he was. They found him. It was time for Diego to split and head to the next area, so his remote was within range of the explosives.

CHAPTER 29

Ariel was on the back of her horse around the curve about nine hundred yards from the tracks, with her Bow ready. The train came around faster than she thought, but to her, it was not a big deal. She aimed the bow and took the shot. The arrow went straight for the engine's cabinet and, in a second, the arrow hit the window of the train. The cabin window of the train was bulletproof, but that morning, the crew leader gave Ariel one of the special, blue-light arrows; these arrows could penetrate almost anything. The arrow sliced through the window, landing in the control cabinet of the train, and an explosive went off. The blast was so powerful that the windows blew out in pieces, the walls and roof had holes in them, and fire was coming out. The blast threw multiple bodies from the train, and she heard the screams of some burning officers. One fell off the back of the cabinet onto the track and got run over by the next train trailer.

As the train slowed, it was time for Diego to get back to work. He pushed the button on the remote from around four hundred yards away. Even he could hear metal hitting metal as the device set on the tracks shot up to the bottom of the cars. Even the Dynasty soldiers heard it and wondered what was happening. It had worked just as the Leading clan warrior had planned. They were right under all three armory cars. The devices landed on the bottom of the cars, and within ten seconds of that, the devices exploded. With so much thrust from the explosion, all three of the armored cars burst into flames, setting the soldiers on top on fire. The train, even slowing down, was still going at hit speed and would get almost half a mile before fully stopping. Diego hit the other button, and explosives on the side of the rail went off. The power of the explosion was enough to derail the train. The train fell on its side, grinding through the prairie dirt and stopping in the grass. The explosion did some damage to the cars, but not enough to ruin or damage the goods inside.

Some dynasty soldiers were climbing out of the windows and side doors of the cars. The warriors could hear the soldiers jumping off the cars and running into the field. The warriors knew no soldiers were to get away. Once the smoke cleared, Raiden and the warriors dropped to the ground, each soldier getting hit in the head with an arrow Ariel and her crew of archers shot while standing in the grass field. It only took a few seconds, and all the soldiers trying to get away were lying dead in the grass.

With the battle over, one warrior took a Gjallarhorn and made a sound that went through the prairie hills, signaling the wagons, trucks, and civilians to come over and get as many of the supplies and weaponry as possible. A dozen wagons and trailers came over the hill and towards the train.

The civilians parked a wagon next to each car. At the end of the twelve wagons came a diesel-fueled truck and an armor-covered SUV vehicle. The truck and SUV were used for the last two things: scrap metal and whatever was in the special car of the train.

The leader instructed most of the warriors to aid civilians, while the three remained on guard against any subsequent trains. The leader and the remaining five warriors walked over to the Special car. Out of the group came a young woman in her early twenties with a device.

As Ariel and Diego joined Raiden, the leader of the warriors walked over and said, "You have done your part. Head back and get your reward." Raiden wanted to know what was in the special car, but he knew confronting the leader would not end well. His hands signaled Ariel and Diego to follow him. They walked through the grass of the prairie to where their horses were standing. As they got on their horses to head back to Gateway, they saw the young woman open the flat device into two pieces and take a wire covered by what the clan called rubber and connect it to the car. How or what she was doing was puzzling to them, but again, it wasn't their business; they all thought and turned around on their horses, taking off back towards Gateway.

CHAPTER 30

As the boat came to the docks in Gateway, it was easy to tell that the crew, including Jennifer, had been disappointed that they didn't stay in The Big Easy extraordinarily long. According to the captain of the tugboat, it was set that there was some precious cargo they could pick up and return to the flatland trade center. That made up for the break only being five days. The captain pointed out that meant they would probably all be getting more money, which made up for the short stay.

They docked the cargo barge right at the spot where it was easy to park and fill up. It looked like the cargo they were going to load up with one of the cargo boats, full of grains. First, they had to let the cargo of filtered water out. The Big Easy was one of the few places along the river with the equipment and ability to create water from the Gulf that was usable. The water on the river was okay, but because of all the radiation from the ancient cities up north along the river, it was easy to tell that drinking it was poisonous to human.

It had amazed Jennifer with the diversity in the Big Easy. To her, even in Gateway, all you saw were different races and types of humans, but in the big easy, it was different. Just docking. She already meant people from all across the world who weren't even fully human. You have the people like what her uncle called the savages in the windy city ruins. But down here they were called Nebulians. The one she ran it to said they were all across the world a lot stayed in the ruins because the radiation from the ruins didn't harm them, so it was easy to stay away from trouble by staying in the ruins. The man said that each set of ruins had a tribe in it. Each tribe had a different purpose or source of income. In the ruins close to Gateway, he had told of them being more like blacksmiths. They guarded the ruins but let some metal hunters find the metal.

Only a small group of humans could metal hunt, and it was only because they or their family had helped the tribe in some way in the past. But no metal left their town. Only the tribe could purchase the metal. But the catch to that was the tribe would pay well and then make some of the best equipment, from weaponry, armory, ammunition, tools, the Gateway metal doors, and support beams for building the high towers. The Nebulians confirmed that the tribe in the windy city ruins was one of the few tribes that acted like bandits and only went after the people who had already dug up the metal.

That made Jessica think of the time her uncle had talked with Diego of Neptune from the trade center, getting metal in a secret, fishy way, as Uncle Raider had said. Even after her talk with the Nebulian, she heard more tales and stories of things of which she had never heard.

As the setup for the staff of the Gateway dock to unload the cargo, it was easy for the crew to tell that it wasn't normal. Most of the people working were not who they saw just a month ago. But they still told them to set up and let the staff take care of the cargo. "I'll get the payment. You guys, go relax." The captain said.

"Yes, sir," the lead crew member replied. The rest of the crew, along with Jennifer, set out to hit the bars. They were planning to get drunk, but not Jennifer. She was out to see if Uncle Raiden and his crew were there.

The crew found the dock bar. It was the only tavern by the river, but according to the crew, it was one of the best bars you could find on the river, no matter where you went. As she walked inside, it was easy for her to see why. Inside were plenty of tables with signs with low bronze coin prices for the drinks. For a big mug of ale, it was only one bronze. In most bars by the docks, it was at least 5 to 10 bronze coins, and even some, like The Big Easy, it was silver coins. Also, for the men, it was noticeable that the people in charge of getting their drinks and food were attractive women. In their early to mid-twenties, they wear pretty light outfits. Their breast and butts were noticeable, and the men loved it. The men of the tavern were loud and clumsy. She had no problem telling who was drunk and who wasn't.

The bar counter was off to the right by the back wall. It was a larger counter with multiple bartenders working at the time, on the ends of the bar, right and left. You could notice a heavy-muscled man standing guard. Light metal armor was visible beneath his basic clothes. Hanging from his belt were gun holsters, three daggers, and over their shoulders were axes. It was obvious that this man you didn't fight if you had your brains still.

Jennifer walked up to one bartender, who wasn't busy, while her friends grabbed a seat and waited for a server to come over and get their orders.

"Hey," Jennifer said.

"How may I help you?" the Bartender replied.

"Have you heard of Raiden, Arial, or Diego being around here?"

"You mean the archangels? If so, yes, they just got back to town?" The thought of getting back to her family was thrilling to Jennifer. She felt tears starting as the happy and painful thought came to her. It was easy for her to feel joy at being back with family soon, but it also opened the door to the rest of her family being gone and never to be seen again.

"Why do you ask?" The bartender asked.

"The archangels are part of my family from Sand Town." The bartender looked shocked, but Jennifer thought that should be normal because of the rumors of how much damage her family had caused to the Dynasty. The bartender turned and waved, and the guard came over.

"My friend Astrid can take you to where they are staying?" the bartender said. To Jennifer, that was amazing. She would see her family soon. She walked over to the guard, who led her through the door that led behind the bar. She could hear in the background the captain telling the crew they had been paid. The captain also asked where Jennifer was. Before a crew member could point to the bar, she was thrown through the doorway into the storage area behind the bar full of whisky and rum barrels, along with the doorway to the kitchen where the food was being made. But what she noticed were the four Shairyn Knights. As she tried to turn and run out into the front of the bar for help, the bar guard grabbed her and pulled her back in front of him, holding her in position. He was too strong for her to break free, even with him using one arm, but she could smell the sleeper hold. As the guard held the towel over her mouth and nose, all she had was the question of why going through her mind.

CHAPTER 31

Lucifer came into the emperor's chamber of command. It was early morning, way before the sun would rise. The chamber was a considerable-sized room with a large rectangular table in the middle of the room. The walls displayed maps of the area around Gateway. There was a little layout of the inside of Gateway, which is just a rough estimate given by the spies in Gateway.

"Emperor, we have some updates," Lucifer said as he came to the table. The emperor stood at the far end, and the other four generals stood around him. In the middle was a 3D holo map of the region. Flat on the table were small touch flat screens, and on the front of the table, by each spot where the generals stood, were USB ports. It was easy to tell from the holo map that the army soldiers were close to the position. And that the spies in Gateway were returning information for a better layout of Gateway.

"Yes, what is the update?" one general asked.

Lucifer inserted a flash drive into the USB port at the end of the table. The holo map immediately turned into an album of pictures and videos of the crashed train out in the prairie southwest of Nova, of the Big Muddy River. It was easy to tell that the generals were shocked and that the situation displayed in front of the emperor outraged him with anger.

"What The fuck happened!!" the emperor shouted out.

Patrol knights discovered that someone had hijacked it about three days earlier. Lucifer answered.

"How is that possible?" the emperor asked.

"The damage from the hijacked shows, whoever the thieves are, that they have good weaponry and armor." The generals wondered how that was possible.

Everyone knew there were some weapons on the illegal market, but from the pictures, nothing that could cause this much damage. The emperor thought of Gateway. It was a higher-up nation in terms of living compared to the people living outside of the city or around the flatlands, but there had been no update or information about them having technology even close to what Nova had.

Lucifer continued, "It looks like the thieves could even break into the system to open the door for the security car of the train." To all the generals, that was impossible. Nova was the only place known to have computer technology at all. There had to be somewhere that was providing the resources, but where and how? The answer was the union to the generals. It was the only Nation that the Dynasty had no information about. It had been almost impossible for spies to get past the boundaries, according to the last report. The union had closed boundaries to the Dynasty and Frozen Kingdom completely.

"Did they take anything else?"

"Yes, sir. They took most of the food, metal, power batteries, and other supplies from the train, too." The emperor thought for a second, which meant they were moving slowly to move all that cargo. This made it quite possible they won't be back in the city until next week. After this mission was done, it would be easy for the Shairyn knights to get the cargo back before the clans had any idea what they had stolen.

To his generals, the emperor asked, "How quickly will the army be in position?"

"It should be all good tomorrow, sir," the top general replies. "With the invasion imminent, the knights' aim is to capture most warriors to prevent any subsequent retaliation." The general said.

To the emperor, this sounded perfect. Tomorrow, it would be under control, and then the Dynasty would have full command.

"What about the bandits? Have we heard anything about them?" the emperor asked.

"From what we have heard, they arrived at Gateway four days ago," Lucifer replies. To the generals and the emperor, that was good. We would finally capture them, too, they thought.

"Any Idea besides being saved what the bandits were doing in Gateway?" one general asked.

"People say that someone ordered them to take part in the train hijacking to repay the clans," Lucifer answered.

The Dynasty's bribing of some clan leaders secured their collaboration. Sadly, revenge motivated most clan leaders, while others were driven by greed. No matter what, it was working great for the emperor to win this battle and cut off a line of resources for the Union.

"You can leave now." One general told Lucifer. Before being completely gone, he heard the emperor give the command that the bandits were to be captured, along with the other warriors of the Clans, tonight.

CHAPTER 32

It had been a beautiful three days on their travel back to Gateway, and early in the evening, they arrived in the city.. It blew their minds that the flatlands outside of the dynasty could be so full of life. From the area they lived in, the Shairyn land, it was drought, and most life didn't grow well in that part of the flatlands, but once you crossed the Big Muddy, things changed. Raiden and his crew arrived at Gateway three days after the hijacking. Today would be the day they could get supplies and more information on the whereabouts of Jennifer.

At this moment, after the long journey down south, one guard in the city had messages from Mangus that confirmed she was still with the crew on the tugboat that had kidnapped her. From what they learned, the tugboat and crew had saved her from the wild, but forced her into slavery on the boat. The last information the guard had was that she and the tugboat crew in Gateway. To Raiden, that meant today they would go to the docks on the Mud River and see about finding Jennifer before the boat left again.

As they arrived at the doorway to Gateway, the Warriors in front of the doorway signaled the soldier inside to open the doors. The giant metal doors opened with a beautiful view of the town. Gateway was still living and running. You could see people walking down the roads, looking through the big front windows of the shops. But the crew knew they had to get to the headquarters of the clan first and see about getting information.

Once into the Gateway, they rode the horse to the stable outside of the headquarters and were pairing to get off and walk to the fence gate to get in and see Mangus to confirm they were done with owing the clans. As they got off and walked their horses to the stables to rest for a little, one of the clan members with the lion sign on his clothing walked into the stable. He was in a basic outfit like the other citizens of Gateway, jeans, a t-shirt, boots, and his scabbards, with a fancy-looking sword in it, which had a bright shine. You could even see a sparkle of gold on the handle of the sword.

"Raiden?" he asked.

"Yes," Raiden answered.

"Impressive. You have made it back." But from the voice, it was easy to tell that this clan leader wasn't so thrilled that they were. He walked over and patted Raiden on the shoulder. "We should celebrate this glorious victory."

To Raiden, that meant they no longer owed the clan. He looked at the others and they all knobbed in agreement on what that meant. "We'll head off and get some supplies and leave you guys alone."

"Are you sure?" the clan member asked.

"Yes, we are, but thanks." Raiden easily sensed that the clan leader had a different agenda, but he wouldn't reveal it now. The headquarters tower was only a few blocks away from the river docks. Making it not an awful choice to let the horses rest for the rest of the day while they went and investigated for more information on Jennifer.

To verify what the lion's clan leader had said, they arrived at the headquarters tower where Mangus was. They walked in and went to the meeting room where Mangus was talking to a fellow member of the Thunder Clan. Raiden noticed that the symbol the man had on his shirt was just like Mangus's. Mangus patted the man on the shoulder, and the man walked away and out of the room.

"Hello," Mangus said. "I heard you were a great help on the mission." They all knobbed yes.. Mangus walked over, patting Raiden on the back. We must celebrate his victory. If you will stay the night, we can celebrate tomorrow." Mangus said.

Raiden thought for a second and figured with searching for Jennifer till they found her staying the night didn't sound bad

Raiden thought to himself "I agree" Raiden said as Mangus walked out of the meeting room and door the hall to a room that looked like his office As walked in and was closed the door. "Get your money with Russel downstairs," he said, "and a celebration we will have," he shouted.

Raiden, Ariel, and Diego went downstairs to Russell's office. Even though Russel was still traveling back with the goods, his secretary sat at the front desk of his office, had the bags of armor and weapons sitting next to them, with warriors in front of the office.,

After a long talk with the secretary, all three arrived at the docks later that night. The docks were busy with barges unloading supplies and materials, while other barges were loading materials and supplies. It was easy to see that most of the people who were working were the workers of the clan, and most of the trader crews were off, with a few just watching. There were just a handful of workers, and you didn't see too many warriors or guards around.

As Raiden, Ariel, and Diego walked around, they could see some barges that arrived on the last day or so.

"Let's split up and ask some of the dock workers if they see or hear anything about Jennifer." Diego and Ariel agreed. Ariel took off towards the tugboats docked on the south side of the docks, and Diego and Raider went up to the north end. Diego went to the first tugboat, and Raiden went to the second. With a few questions from the workers, it was easy to say that they had not seen or heard anything about Jennifer. They ended up being close to the bar, and it would be a good place to stop and see who was there.

Inside the Tavern, it was easy to tell that the sizeable crowd over at the counter was a crew from one boat. That group was most of the crowd. It looked like most tradesmen and tugboat sailors were gone. They could hear the group laughing and cheering.

"How's it going?' Diego asked as he walked over to their table. The sailors looked surprised and unhappy that he was even talking to them.

"What do you want?' one sailor asked.

"I am wondering if you guys have seen or heard of a young woman named Jennifer?" The Sailors looked surprised and suspicious of him, asking about Jennifer, which was a good sign that they knew something.

"Why do you care?" one sailor asked.

"I am her uncle Diego."

"Prove it." That was going to be a little hard for most people out in the flatlands, but Diego was one of the few who got tattoos made on his body. On his left upper arm were tattoos of the names of his boys, Diego Jr. and Daniel, and his nephew and niece, Robert and Jennifer. Without hesitation, Diego pulled up his sleeve and showed the crew the tattoos.

The captain of the crew answers, "Yes, we know Jennifer. She is the cook of the boat." To Diego, this was the best thing he could have ever heard.

"Do you know where she is?

"No. She came to the bar with us but disappeared. We figured she was more in the city, looking for you all. She talks about the archangels as her family all the time." So, she and the crew already knew that Diego, Ariel, and Raiden were the archangels. All three were hoping she never had to hear that or ever have to deal with that. Now the question is, are they lying, or is it true?

"What's the name of your boat?"

"Why do you need to know?" one of the crew members asks.

"Just curious."

"Curious or not, go fuck off." The entire crew waved at him to get lost. "Also, remind her if you find her, she has a contract and needs to be back here by dawn." One member said.

To Diego, that didn't matter. Only finding Jennifer was what mattered. Diego walked up to Raiden, who was talking to a few other people at the bar counter. It was some older men who you could tell were regulars at the tavern. Close to being super drunk soon and out cold not long after. Diego tapped Raiden on the shoulder. "I have some good news."

Raiden's eyes glowed with joy as he heard that. He thanked the men and patted them on the back, leaving a gold coin on the bar counter, and told the bartender that it was for the old men. The old men were enthusiastic, knowing they could now get some free ale.

"What's the good news?" Raiden asked.

"Jennifer's here," Diego answered.

"That is amazing." Raiden replied, then he asked, "Where?"

Diego turns slightly, looking over at the group of men. "That is the tradesman who took her after the attack. They say she left a couple of hours ago and doesn't know where she is." Diego could see the fury on Raider's face. It was easy for Diego to tell that Raiden was going to start a fight soon.

"Hey, calm down. We will deal with them later; we must find Jennifer first." To Raiden, that was the truth. They had to find Jennifer first, before they had anything else to do with the crew. But Raiden was determined that this wasn't over.

"I found out that she was asking around about us," Raiden said. That made sense to Diego.

"So, she is asking about us, but where is she now?" Diego asked.

"The bartender says she left, heading more into town, looking for us," Raiden replied.

"Okay, let's go get Ariel and then head into town."

"Sounds good," Raiden said. "I'll deal with those asses later."

As they walked out of the tavern, they ran into Ariel. "She is here somewhere," Raiden told Ariel.

Ariel's face was just as obvious as Raiden's face of how happy she was to hear it. They were determined to find Jennifer tonight at all costs.

CHAPTER 33

The small boat came out of the fog, late at night, with some light still coming over the wall of Gateway. Normally, there were barbed wire and naval bombs in the river, but the clans of the city that Lucifer and the dynasty were working with had shut off the system, for the moment, to let him and a few of his soldiers in as he returned to the city to finish the plan of invasion. Half a dozen squads sent by him had already entered the city to move through it and capture warriors, leaders, and especially the bandits rumored to be in Gateway. That way, they could not interfere with the rest of Lucifer's army the next morning.

It was still a little surprising that the Lions clan and its allies would work with the Dynasty after all the battles they had had, but these clans were not loyal to anyone besides themselves. With the bride for the power of the Gateway and gold, the three clans had agreed without hesitation. To most people, it was sad that these clans were so foolish to trust the dynasty. But to Lucifer, it was just the perfect job for him to fool them into believing that the dynasty would trust them to be in charge of the city after they backstabbed their own fellow citizens. This last meeting would put the full mission into motion, Lucifer thought.

The boat came to the wall of the city. looked like the boat would crash right into it, and they would all fall into the strong current of the mud river, with no chance of survival. But the boat went through the wall in the small docking tunnel. It amazed Lucifer; this was technology even the dynasty itself had yet to have. Lucifer thought the dynasty would gain another treasure after the invasion ended. The boat came to the edge of the dock with two warriors standing guard and a longshoreman ready to help. The longshoreman grabbed the side of the boat. He was tall and looked muscular, pulling the boat over. He took the dock line from the boat and wrapped it around the mooring, securing the boat to the dock. The longshoreman stood back, and the two warriors went over to help Lucifer on the dock. Once on the dock, the other warrior showed Lucifer to the stairway up into the city. Atop the stairway stood a family member of the serpent clan. He greeted Lucifer and walked him out into a hall. There stood the group of lion clan warriors and the leader of the lion clan.

The old man stood tall, looking strong for an eighty-year-old person. It was still phenomenal that this man had lived to be eighty. Most people who lived outside of the big cities like Nova only lived to be sixty at the latest, and that itself was extremely rare.

"Hello, Charles," Lucifer said, putting his hand out to shake.

Charles did the same. "Is your army ready for this?" Charles asked.

"Indeed, it is Charles. The army will move whenever you're ready."

"Good. We will gather the other clan warriors tonight." Charles replied. Perfect, thought Lucifer. Once Lucifer and the clans rounded up the warriors of the other clans and the show was done, the army could take over the entire city, and he could get rid of this greedy, backstabbing family for good. Lucifer knew that this family was not to be trusted. Greed drove them, with no exception.

CHAPTER 34

It had been hours since they talked to the tugboat crew at the tavern about finding Jennifer. They had found nothing else. All the other taverns and shops they made it to before closing had no clue about a girl named Jennifer. It was hard for Raiden to even think of sitting down or sleeping with the idea that Jennifer was in this town now. But he was exhausted, and it looked like Ariel and Diego were the same. He stopped by one of the corner lights at the end of the block. He could easily see that Gateway residents slept little. Just a block away was the downtown area. There were open taverns with plenty of people in them. But Raiden did not want to check the taverns out. To him, it would not help him find his niece.

Diego sat down on a bench next to a large flowerpot set right on the edge of the sidewalk. Ariel was standing up, stretching her arms. You could hear the crackling noises her arms made from down the block.

"That had to hurt?" Diego

"Ha, no Diego, you ass. It felt good. "Raiden noticed that both Ariel and Diego were exhausted and needed to rest. He felt like fainting right there himself because of how much energy his mind had used up in the last 5 hours. His mind had been jumping from scenario to scenario about what the outcome was going to be tonight, and this was the one outcome he did not want. He was sure now that he would not find Jennifer tonight.

"Ok, let's go get a bed at the inn away from the taverns." Both Ariel and Diego agreed it was time to get some rest. They would check up on the tugboat crew tomorrow before they took off, just in case Jennifer had returned. There was an Inn close to the river that would make it easier for them to catch the crew in the morning. It took them over forty minutes to get to the Inn, and it was obvious that once you got away from the business area, most other people were resting for the night. The inn still had a door light on to mark that it was still open. As they walked up to the front, it was easy to see that this was a rundown inn and cost little to stay in. But it did not matter to any of them. They had been sleeping on the ground for most of the last six months or more. A bed of almost any kind would be a relief to them. Once inside, the building had a good-looking interior. Raiden could see the furniture with fine finish cushions on the seats. A fireplace that let out a good warm feeling, and lights that lit up the room. But bright enough to bother anyone. The front desk staff saw them walk in and were ready to find out what they needed.

"How may I help?" the staff asked.

"We need two bedrooms." The staff walked over to their desk to check what was available for the night.

"I am sorry, sir. But we only have two beds with a sofa room left." Raiden was not thrilled, but he knew a sofa would still be better than lying on the ground again. Still, it was weird that the inn would be full of people. There were only two other horses outside. The crew of the river boats never stayed at the inns; only guests were on the boats. All the boats at the docks now were tugboats with no passengers besides the crew.

Raiden put down five gold coins on the countertop.

"It is a little more expensive, sir." But to Raiden, that did not matter. They still had plenty of gold and silver left from just the last metal sale, not counting what they could find that Raiden had stashed away under his sister's farm home.

They had gotten plenty of coins, the only pictures left of his family, and his journal. Raiden took out two gold coins and laid them on the counter, assuming that was more than enough. "Another three, sir. It costs ten gold to stay here." To Raiden, that was ridiculous, but they needed to sleep and be close to the boats. He said nothing but just frowned and gave an unsatisfied face to the front deskman as he laid down the other three coins.

The front deskman scooped them up right away and handed over an iron key to Raiden. Raiden grabbed it, still frustrated with the situation, but knew that sleep would calm him down.

"Return the key by ten tomorrow morning, please."

Whatever, Raiden thought as he looked around to see where the hall door was.

"Sir, it is down this way, to your right." Just the deskman's voice was pissing off Raiden, but he knew a fight right now was a waste of time and he just needed to rest. They walked down the hall, and at the end, there was a fancy-looking door with a clan symbol on it. It was a sign of the lion's clan. Raiden could remember the man who had gotten up to protest them going on the mission was wearing a Lion's clan symbol necklace.

As they walked in, it was extremely easy to tell that what you saw outside of this building was just camouflage. They had already seen an amazing entry, fireplace, furniture, and front desk, not counting the front deskman. But this room was far beyond what they expected. Silk partly made up the curtains, and lion's fur blankets covered the two beds. The pillows on top looked extremely fluffy. The sofa was long and wide, like a third bed. There were beautiful paintings on the walls, along with thick oak wood tables and nightstands next to each bed. The floor was wooden, but its finish and sealant suggested years of lasting beauty.

"Wow," Diego said after landing on one bed. "This is the best bed I've ever slept on."

Raiden knew Diego would not move until the next morning. Ariel was already on the sofa with her face aimed at the door and a dagger in her right hand in case of an invasion that night. Raiden kicked off his boots and put his gun on the nightstand, and his other weapons leaned against the stand. It was time for some rest; He lay down on the bed, and it was a rush of pleasure at how comfortable it was. He almost fell asleep instantly, hearing Diego snoring loudly like normal, which usually kept him up, but not tonight. Tonight was a get rest and nothing less night, he thought.

CHAPTER 35

Raiden woke up to a creaking sound. He rolled over in bed to see what was happening, still half asleep. He caught Ariel slowly moving across the floor of the room. She heard Raiden make some noise rolling over and immediately looked at him, putting one finger over her mouth, informing him to be quiet.

Raiden knew this was not good. Ariel had always had a sensitive ear at night, when during the day she felt something was not right or made little sense to her. When she got up to the door, she leaned over, putting her ear to the door. She could hear some people struggling and marching down the hall. Then, a commander gave some kind of order to what she summed as his soldiers. But what was the clan up to tonight? It was easy for her to tell this was not something normal because of the tone of the people's voices who were being marched down the hall to what she supposed was the entryway of the inn.

She lifted her head, looking back at Raiden, who had put back on his combat boots and was putting back on his holster belt with his gun and ammo on it. She signaled him to wake up Diego and do it quietly. Raiden slowly walked over to Diego, who was sleeping on his right side, snoring a little. Raiden pushed his shoulder and shook Diego a little to wake him up. When Diego woke up, his face signaled he was not happy. But Raiden signaled him to be quiet, and with that, Diego knew something was not right. He did the same as Raiden had and put on his boots, Holst, and rifle sling. He left the duffle bag with the bigger weapons, ammo, and explosives on the floor because they would make too much noise moving right now.

Ariel heard the last of the footsteps move down the hall into the lobby of the inn. She could hear a command and more soldiers. This meant to her that the soldiers knew she and her companions were the only ones left in the rooms and were gathering reinforcements before attacking their room. She hand-signed Raiden and Diego that it was time to move forward and out of the room. She opened the room door slowly, then stuck her head out to check for anyone in the hall. Diego picked up the bag, and Raiden grabbed his backpack; Diego signaled to Raiden to catch and throw over the extra assault rifle he had. Ariel had already gotten her quiver and bow. She crouched down in the hall with her bow and arrow aimed down the hall to where the soldiers would come from. She signaled Raiden and Diego to move out. They both came out of the room with assault rifles ready to fire.

Once they were all out of the room, Raiden looked around for a way to get out of the building, making no noise. It was easy for Raiden to tell that the soldier's plan all along was for them to be pinned at the end of the hall. It was a dead end with no windows or extended hall, just the other room across the hall. Raiden signaled Diego to see about unlocking it.

Over the last year, Diego had learned to unlock the doors from a theft they saved from being caught by a small group of Dynasty soldiers. They were looking for him because he had stolen their stash of money a couple of nights before. Diego had become good at it over the years and could open the door. He signaled the others to follow him in. Inside the room, it was not an inn room; it was more of a utility room with all the cleaning supplies and about a quarter of the size of their room. But they still could all fit in. They got in quietly, and Ariel was the last to enter. And slowly closed the door behind her, making no extra noise.

They all looked around for a window or some kind of way to get out of the inn without being noticed. Raiden noticed on the ceiling of the room that there was a square piece of wood with a small rope hanging from it. Raiden lightly said, "Hey," as he pointed up at the ceiling. Diego and Ariel looked up. Raiden reached up to the rope, but was not tall enough to reach it. He pointed at Diego, who was much taller, to try. Diego had no problem reaching it and pulling the rope. Diego had to jump back a little as the square swung open and a small ladder slid down from the opening. Raiden walked over, putting his assault rifle back into the sling. He stepped up the ladder to check. It was a small attic. He could tell they were going to have to commando crawl through the attic. He could see a pathway across the attic floor made of sturdy wood that was normally used to make walls. Meaning it would be strong enough to hold them for now.

Raiden raised his thumbs, signaling to Ariel and Diego that it was good. And finished climbing up the ladder and got into the commando crawl position. And started down the small pathway in the attic. Ariel fit in perfectly, just having to put the bow and quiver over her shoulders and onto her back. But for Diego, this would not be simple. He climbed up, looked at the situation, and stepped back down. He took the duffle bag handle and adjusted the length as much as possible. He then took it and put it over his back. It hung down to his legs, and then he climbed up the ladder. Once he was in position, he could tell it was going to be a little rough, but the bag could still move with him as he crawled on the wooden pathway.

It took only a few minutes after getting up before they heard the soldiers moving down and kicking the door to the room they had been in for the night. Their puzzled reaction to the noise prompted them to signal the commander to investigate. They could all tell when the commander had arrived and checked out of the room. They understood one hundred percent that he was furious when he screamed out, "FIND THEM, NOW!"

CHAPTER 36

The captain of the old tugboat woke up to hear a noise of some kind going on outside the boat, in a possible neighboring boat. He got up, still in uniform, and headed up the stairs to the deck of the boat. One of the crew members should have woken him up by now because there was a noise like this going on. But as he got up, he saw the crew member sitting in a position on the deck, leaning against the wall on the edge of the deck, facing the water of the river, snoring.

This ass is getting disciplined, the captain thought. The captain walked over to the sailor and kicked him in the legs as he lay leaning against the rail. The young man woke up startled, but soon became worried when they realized it was the captain who woke them up.

"What do you think you are doing? You are supposed to be on guard tonight, George."

"Sorry, Sir,"

"Sorry, does not matter. What matters at hand is that I need you to wake up the crew quietly. Something is going on." George stood up and headed down the stairs to the bunks where the other crew members were. The captain looked over onto the docks and could see other boats where crews were being walked out of their boats by dynasty knights. What was the dynasty doing here? This was an invasion, but how? The captain thought. The clan armies would never let this happen. That is when he saw one of the clan leaders walk up to one knight. He looked at the edge of the boat to see if they were about to take off, and he could see the dock chains connected to his boat with a strong-looking padlock needing a key to unlock it. He looked out into the river to see if they could leave and easily saw that large metal chains connected the dock to his boat. Due to: Chains connected to the dock prevented departure, blocking any boat until they were removed.

The crew came up dressed and ready to sail away. The captain stopped and commanded in a whisper that sailors needed to grab all weapons and supplies they could and evacuate the boat immediately. Once all the bows and arrows, spears, a few rifles, handguns, and supplies the sailors could gather were done. The captain pointed to a spot on the dock that led to the storage area for material that was brought in. It was easy to see the four Knights standing guard, but the captain was confident his crew would not have a problem getting past them. The crew got on the dock and could see that the other boat sailors were being escorted off in handcuffs and chains connecting each sailor.

It was a pity that those sailors were like that, but the captain did not have time to help other boats and their crews. He and his crew needed to get to safety. He pointed at one of his sailors with one of the long-distance bows. The crew member knobbed and took out the special arrows they had gotten down in The Big Easy at a sale of special weaponry. He took the Bow and Arrow, aiming at the Knight who was in charge, they believed, and shot the arrow. It went through the air silently, twenty feet before getting close to the knights and splitting into four spikes while in the air. The spikes landed right into the chest of the Knights. They jerked back when the arrows almost penetrated the armor, but before the knights could say anything, a blast of electricity jumped between the solid connections to each spike. Even from a distance, the crew could see the waves of electricity jumping between the knights. It only took a few seconds, and then the knights all fell to the ground.

In the distance from the inn, they heard a commander yell something, and a handful of the soldiers ran inside the building to see what was going on. Leaving only about a dozen Knights on the dock in front of the inn.

As the crew got closer to the group of knights they had killed, they noticed that the warehouse where the material went was full and that the surrounding walkway led to a dead end dropping off into the river. Shit, the captain thought and looked back at the inn and bar close to it. There was a high brick wall behind each building, along with the wall extending to the warehouse where they were, with only a few ladders on the wall between the warehouse and the inn. Someone had mounted guns and spear guns on the wall's edge, but they appeared unoccupied.

Carts used daily by salesmen to sell various items to the crews were between the warehouse and the tavern. The captain also saw that around the Inn was a road that led up a hill. The captain thought the road probably connected to the rest of the city, and, given the inn's event, they could use the sales carts as cover to ambush the soldiers outside.

The captain explained to the crew. In groups of three, the captain and two of the crew moved first, slowly and quietly moving one cart forward at a time. As groups of three, they could fit behind each cart, and the crew of twelve sailors moved forward in stealth to the inn.

The captain saw more knights walk into the inn and away from the group of chained prisoners. Leaving only six knights on guard. The captain still had no clue how many besides the twelve knights he saw go into the inn were there altogether, but the six outside right now, he knew he could take care of.

The captain put up his hand, signaling the crew to stop moving any closer. They were in the closest position possible without being noticed. He hand signaled the sailor with the special arrows to shoot the last electric arrow, and the other two sailors with a bow to shoot. The sailor with the special arrow again shot it, again splitting it into four, hitting the knights in the chest and electrocuting them. As the other two knights noticed their fellow knights dropping to the ground, they took guard and were about to shout out to the other knights for help when an arrow with a blue glow in the front sliced through their armor and landed in their chest. Puncturing their lungs, making them incapable of shouting out for help. They stumbled and landed on the ground, gasping for air and bleeding to death.

After that, the captain gave the Signal to move forward at full speed to get to the hill and out of the docking area. As they were getting closer, it was easy to tell the group of prisoners were sailors, the sales associates of the carts they hid behind, and some basic civilians who were there at the wrong time. The captain knew by the code of tradesmen on the mud river that you should always help another tradesman. The captain signaled two of his crew members to see if he could unchain the other sailors and people. The rest of the crew took guard in the doorway to ambush any other knight who came outside.

CHAPTER 37

As Raiden and his friends reached the roof louver, he could hear something going on outside. It sounds like a light zap, and then it bumps like something fell to the ground. If anything, it was a distraction from the sound he made opening the louver, which was a top hinge, and an exceedingly small, weak chain link locked on the bottom. It would not be hard to get out. Raiden connected the grip hook to the edge of the wall and lowered the rope close to the ground. He needed to turn around, so he lowered himself down onto the rope. He gave the instructions for the others to back up a little, and he went backward. Once his legs were out, he lowered them so they were against the wall of the building, and then slowly slid out holding the rope. Giving the signal to Ariel and Diego to follow. Once he was fully out of the building, he lowered himself to the ground. Not long after, Ariel and Diego were with him. There was a window a little further forward, which looked into the lobby of the inn.

Raiden took a sneak peek through the window. It looked like around six warriors were by the front door, waiting for commands from the sergeant in charge of the group. They were dynasty knights. The clans would never agree with that. But then he saw a Clan leader wearing the Lions sign on the inn room door they had stayed in that night, talking to the Sergeant. It was like Raiden had thought; it was the clan leader who had protested about them collaborating with the clans on the train hijacking mission.

Now it was making a little more sense. But it could not just be one clan; there must be multiple clans working together. Then the question came up: why would clans be working with the dynasty? There had to be a reason for all this to happen, but it did not matter to Raiden. Getting his niece and going home was the plan right now. Nothing else really mattered.

Raiden pointed towards the front of the building to let the rest know he was moving. He sneaked up to the front edge of the building and looked around the corner. To Raiden's surprise, he saw dynasty knights lying on the ground. And some people freed the other people the dynasty had captured from a chain line. The man doing so looked familiar, but Raiden could not figure out why. Off to the side were the horse stables. Raiden figured they would grab their horses if they were still there and then take off.

It looked like the group of people freeing the other people were good, but the last thing was to start a conflict or somehow make too much noise and have the soldiers from inside the inn notice them. The stable was just a few feet away from the inn. They could get there without a problem, but once they got in view of the stables, they noticed the horses were gone. Someone had taken the horses. Now, Raiden, Ariel, and Diego could not just ride past the crowd with no worry. They would now have to confront the people in front of the building, along with trying to avoid the knights who were inside the inn searching for them.

"We are going to have to meet these people," Raiden explained.

"Why?" Ariel asked. Raiden knew Ariel's question was why not just kill them?

"Because there is no way to sneak around the building. The road going into town is the only way away from the dock."

"What about all the knights in the inn?" asked Ariel. That was a good question, Diego and Raiden thought. Raiden knew the knights would find out how they got out of the building and would be outside the inn soon.

"Follow my lead," Raiden said as he put his gun back into the holster, Ariel, sighed in frustration but still put her bow over her shoulder. Diego did the same with his rifle over his shoulder and zipped up the bag, so it was closed. All three walked out of the stable in plain sight, making it easy for the people in charge to see them. A few raised their rifles and aimed. Ariel immediately was ready to grab her bow and arrows, but Raiden put his arm in front of her to signal her to stand down. Again, she sighed in frustration, but followed the command.

As they got closer to the group of people, it was easy to tell it was the sailors they met at the tavern the other day, the crew Jessica worked with. The sailors recognized Raiden, Ariel, and Diego right away, too.

But before they talked, they heard a command of some sort from the Sergeant inside the inn, and immediately afterward, two Knights came out of the front door of the inn. With Sailors standing by the door ready, the Knights were only out of the inn before being ambushed and killed. But that was the signal to the sailors and Raiden's crew. It was time to leave. The captain gave a signal for the crew to leave. The sailor, a skilled locksmith, freed the captured people.

The sailors and a group of other fellow sailors and civilians followed the command and headed up the road on the hill. Raiden and the Crew followed, too. They had reached the top of the hill. When they all could hear the Sergeant shouting out a command again, even though they did not fully hear the command, they all could tell he was not happy and that the knights would be up and after them in only a few minutes. They had to find shelter and a place to hide.

The group all looked around for somewhere to hide. They were in one of the city's business plazas. It was an open space with businesses all on the edge of the plaza. From the signs hanging in front of all the buildings it was easy to tell that this plaza was full of bakeries, general supply stores, actual candy stores, tailors and seamstress stores, multiple restaurants, and even a few blacksmith stores but what caught Raiden's eye was a bakery that on the sign was specifically for breakfast food only, with its lights on. The captain saw it too and pointed to it. They moved towards it. The sign on the door was an open sign. The group moved in. It was a decent-sized bakery. There were a handful of wooden tables for people to sit at and eat their breakfast. Abstract art was all across the left wall, and off to the right side was the counter with shelves with glass in front showing dozens of types of donuts, muffins, bread, bagels, biscuits, Danish rolls, and cinnamon rolls. The food looked delicious. Small signs displaying the prices of the food items were on top of the shelves. Behind the counter was an open space and then a right-hand wall with a chalkboard on it, with the sales of the day written all over it in big colorful letters.

As the group entered the building, a little bell on top of the door rang. You could hear a woman behind the counter saying. "I will be with you soon."

Just as everyone was inside the bakery, the woman stood up from behind the counter, startled by how many people were in the building already. As she was about to say something, the captain interrupted, "Madam, we all need to hide, you included."

"What, why? What's Going on?!" the lady asked. The captain did not have time to explain this. He looked over at Ariel, who was locking the front door and turning the open sign around to close. A few of the crew members escorted the civilians into the shop. While the captain was trying to explain to the store owner the danger she was in. Diego had slid back behind the counter and found the switch for the lights in the building, and with a quick flick of his finger, the power was out, and the store looked closed.

Just as the lights went out, a group of twelve knights showed up on the plaza. They looked around for a difference in the environment but could not find any immediately. Following not far behind was the Sergeant. He was in a state of fury. The three people he was supposed to have captured were gone, and there was a chance that more people would know about the invasion now.

Most of the people had hidden in the back of the bakery, but Ariel, Raiden, the captain, and the bakery lady stayed up front and kneeled behind the counter, peeking over to see if any knights came close. From their point of view, they saw all the knights arrive and spread out. They had all split into couples. Six couples in total, each one looking through the windows of the buildings and searching alleys for any clue where the bandits and prisoners had gone.

"We meet again."

"Yes, we do, Captain….??"

"You can call me Captain Pens."

"Well, Capt. Pens, I am Raiden."

"So, do you know how we got into this mess?"

"Not really. My crew and I woke up to knights escorting other sailors off their boats. We were lucky to be awake in time to notice, or we would have been the prisoners, too."

The group of knights was searching around the plaza, but because of the secrets they wanted to keep about their investigation, they did not get into any of the businesses. They would check the windows and see if their front door was open. One of the Knights came to the front door of the Bakery. They looked in to see if they noticed anything going on. Raiden, Ariel, Capt. Pen and the lady who owned the bakery ducked behind the counter. Having checked the door to see if it was locked, they heard the knight walk away from the front door.

"What do we do now?" Capt. Pen asked.

"We have to figure out what is going on and warn the leader of the clans that the Lions clan is working with the dynasty."

"How do we do that?" Ariel asked, and with that question, Raiden figured, like himself, no one knew exactly what to do now. But the Bakery lady knew more about this city than any of the sailors, Ariel, or Raiden.

"What's your name?" Raiden asked the bakery lady.

"Susan."

"Do you know where the clan leader lives and anything about the Lions?"

"Yes, our leader of the clan of thunder, the name is Magnus. And the leader of the Lions clan is Charles MacKean." The necessity of explaining the names annoyed Susan. But Raiden could tell that she was even more frustrated with the whole situation altogether. "Charles is such a baby. He and the Lions clan are corrupt. They lost in the clan voting of who the leader of all the Clans was, even though they are the biggest clan in Gateway. Making so the lions were not in charge like they wanted." It made sense why the clan would be mad, but could they work with the Dynasty?

"Does their working with the Dynasty make sense at all?" Raiden asked.

"One hundred percent. It makes sense. All the Dynasty had to say was that the Lions were in charge once they had control of Gateway." It still puzzled Raiden that anyone would work with the Dynasty after all he and his friends had seen over the last year. The dynasty had been killing villagers and destroying entire towns because of people not paying enough in taxes. Sometimes it was not even really the Dynasty itself, it was just the Knights and Sergeants punishing towns for stuff, just like what they did to his family back in Sand Town. Justification for what the Lions were doing was unnecessary; that was for Mangus to figure out, not Raiden.

"Okay, we need to tell Mangus about what's going on."

"Susan, do you know where Mangus could be right now?"

"At home. He lives next to the Glass Tower, where the Clan leaders meet. His house will have the Clan of Thunder sign on the front door." Susan handed a piece of paper with a symbol of what Raiden thought was a Warhammer. Raiden knew exactly where the Class tower was, and they would have to find the building with the sign of a Warhammer on the front door.

"Arial and I will head to the Mangus house, but can you see if a few sailors would like to join us, just in case we run into the knights again?" Raiden asked Capt. Pen, Capt. Pen shook his head yes and went back into the kitchen to see who would join Raiden and Ariel. Raiden figured Diego should stay and help the rest of the sailors and civilians set up barricades at the doorways to the bakery for safety, in case the knights came back again.

"We are going to be setting up barricades in case the Knights come back," Raiden told Susan.

"Sounds good to me, but I hope I get the chance to help with the fight." Raiden noticed that ever since they had met the Gateway people, they were always open for fights, especially fights that had a chance of death involved in it. Pens came back up with a few members of his crew and a couple of other members of the other two crews.

"These guys jumped right in when I asked," Pen said with a smirk on his face. Giving the signal that he had already known that he would not have a problem finding people to help Raiden and Ariel.

"Good. Who do we have joining?"

The sailors all said their names, Travis, John, Roger, Richard, who said to call him dick, and one sailor said Popeye. All five of them had weapons. Travis and John both had bows and arrows along with a belt with a handful of daggers connected to it and a holster for a revolver handgun with a pouch on the side filled with packs of bullets. Roger and Popeye had assault rifles and Dick with a belt covered in handgun magazines for a Glock 17, along with a Saif sword over his shoulder looking like what some people of the Forbidden Land used when they invaded villages close to the edge of the desert.

"Let's find Mangus!" Raiden told the group. To Raiden, this would make it so that the Clans owe them now instead of them owing the Clans.

CHAPTER 38

Magnus sat in an old craftsman wooden chair carved with writings and designs depicting the tales of Thor, the god of thunder—a powerful warrior figure in history, though not necessarily a true one. Even if the tales the elderly talked about were just stories and nothing else. It was the living room of his home, which neighbored the Glass Tower where he and the council met. His home was a basic home with Warhammer, and swords across it along with a few heads of beast he had hunted down over the years but his prize trophy was the body arm of the great dynasty general Omen covered with bloodstains and with a hole in the armor where Mangus's grandfather, over a hundred years ago had thrust his spear into Omen's chest killing and winning the great battle that stopped the dynasty from ever getting close to this part of the Muddy River again. It was how the clans fully became a nation and were no longer under the dynasty's control.

A middle-aged man from the Lions clan stood in front of Mangus, looking at him. "So, it was your grandfather?" the lion's member asked.

Mangus did not reply. To Mangus, this petty young man of the lion's clan did not deserve a word from him, after what this man had done to fellow Gateway warriors and against Mangus's wife, Thyra. To Mangus, the killing of his wife without the chance for her or anyone to defend her was the most dishonorable action a lion's clan member could do. Just seeing the sword leaning against the wall with her blood still dripping onto the floor. It was infuriating to Mangus and his children.

The young man turned around, looking over at the group of dynasty knights waiting. The leading member shook his head no.. The young man waved for two of the soldiers to come over. "Find Lucifer. Now!"

It was easy for Mangus to notice that the young man was impatient. "What's your name?" Mangus asked.

"You talk now. As the leader of the clans, I would have figured you would know the influential members of the great Lions Clan."

"Great lions," Mangus said with a little chuckle. To him, the lion's clan was a laugh. After years of corruption and dishonor, the governing board of clans had decided they had had enough and voted for one of the original clans of the nation to lead the clans again.

"How dare you laugh, you pathetic coward? You are not a genuine leader. My Grandfather is a leader and will be the official leader of Gateway soon." That comment points out to Mangus that it was not just some clan members who were betraying Gateway, but the entire clan. And their potent allies, too, Mangus thought.

Just as the young man was about to go on about how the Lion's clan was better than the Thunder clan, a man wearing a dark leather hooded cloak walked into the living room. As he entered, all the dynasty knights raised their hands, putting them into a fist and beating their armor chests three times. All in a deep voice said, "Sir." The man did the same and waved his hand for them to leave the room. With this staff and the knights' actions, Mangus could tell this was a high-ranking member of the dynasty army.

"Hello, Duke of the Lions." The grin across the young man's face could tell anyone who addressed him as the Duke that he wasn't a devoted follower of the lion's clan, where ego and greed were always the motivation.

"Lucifer, it is late."

"I apologize. It had taken me longer than expected to get here from Nova. "To the Duke, it did not matter at all why, just that Lucifer was late. Lucifer walked up to the duke and whispered in his ear. "Fine, take Mangus to the Tower. Find out what you need, but he must be ready for his execution on the city stage tomorrow afternoon…" With that being said, Lucifer whistled, and the

Knights returned to the room. Lucifer told the two to stay with the duke while he tried to interrogate Mangus's daughter and son, who sat next to Mangus in their own two chairs from the dinner room set.

Both of Mangus's kids looked confused and upset about the situation, but both understood that this time was not the time to let those thoughts and feelings be let out. "DON'T YOU DARE TOUCH MY CHILDREN!" Mangus shouted.

The duke acted like the anger was nothing and waved at Mangus to shut up. With no hesitation, Mangus jumped up and ran, slamming into the duke. He still held onto the wooden chair. The chair broke into pieces as the force of Mangus's movement collided with the duke and the wall. Before Mangus cleared his thoughts, he stood up and fought. Lucifer had already signaled his group of knights to take him down. Four knights slammed him into the wall to knock over a few of these trophies. Two on each side pinned his arms to the wall, and the leading knight came up and punched Mangus in the gut.

Mangus felt the pain and lost his grasp on the air. He coughed, leaning forward, clearing his head, and getting ready to fight back, but the leading knight swung, punching him in the face. Mangus could feel the blood coming down his face, but the anger was blocking the pain. The Leader lifted Mangus's head to see the full effect of the punch. Mangus slammed his forehead into the leader's face with all his might. The blow was simply perfect in that it made the leader's mind foggy, and he lost balance, stumbling back and falling to the ground. Without a single thought, one knight holding Mangus's right arm let go and tried to catch the leading knight before he hit the ground. The three others looked back in shock that he did that, and it was the perfect moment for Mangus to pull his arm free, pushing the knights holding on away. With another thrust of energy, he head-butted another knight. With only one knight left, Mangus swung his fist around, sucker punching the last soldier on the side of his face. The sucker punch was right on the spot, making the knight stumble back, falling to the ground out cold.

Quickly, Mangus grabbed a sword he had for triumph off the wall and lunged forward to stab the duke. The duke was terrified by this whole situation. The fear was easy to see, and it backed up Mangus's belief that the lion's clan members were all cowards. Before the sword could reach the duke, a Knight's sword slammed against Mangus in defense of the duke. With the chance, the duke ran into the other room and signaled his soldiers to go in and kill Mangus.

CHAPTER 39

The normal warriors who took guard of the glass building where those clan meetings were not on guard. Instead, it was the Lion clan warriors, and walking into the building were dynasty knights. They were different soldiers. To Ariel, she was sure it was Shairyn Defense Warriors along with basic Shairyn Knights. Once the group of dynasty knights was inside, it was time for the group to move towards the home of the thunder clan, where Mangus lived. But first, they had to pass the warriors at the gateway to the glass tower. Raiden and the two sailors with bows moved forward, kneeling behind a tall, about six feet wide, rock flower bed with small bushes of flowers. Raiden signaled the sailors to take down the warriors. Both Travis and John aimed, shot, and, without a sound, had the two warriors fall to the ground after the arrows landed on the faces of the warriors. Raiden now knew these sailors were better than he expected them to be.

Raiden waved at Ariel and the rest of the sailors to move forward with him. Once the entire group was behind the flowerbed. Raiden pointed at the other couple of flowers, like the one they were behind, that followed along the walls of the city square where the glass tower was located. They split into three groups, two groups of two and one group of three. Ariel was in the group of three at the end, and Raiden was in the first group with Travis. With the warriors down at the gate, it was not too difficult to move around to the other side of the city square, but being cautious would not hurt.

Signaling the two sailors with Ariel to get the bodies of the warriors and bring them behind one of the flower beds. Once the bodies were over, it was obvious to Raiden that the sailors, Roger and Popeye, could easily fit the armor. Raiden pointed at the armory, and, with no need to explain, the two sailors undressed the warriors and put the armor on themselves. Once they wore the armor, Raiden pointed to the steps near the Thunder Clan home. Both sailors walked over and took a stand at the right and left corners of the steps to the door of the building. With the sailors set in place to watch the guard and keep traffic away from the house, the rest of the group moved over.

As they moved closer to Mangus's home, they could hear chaos breaking out inside the building. Raiden quickly looked in one of the front windows of the building, seeing Mangus battling a group of dynasty knights. Raiden could not tell the full size of the group and who was all in there, but he knew they had to make sure Mangus was still alive if the clans were going to owe them a reward of any kind.

"We have to help Mangus now," Raiden told the group. With no hesitation, Raiden, Ariel, and the group of sailors moved in, busting through the front door. Raiden told the two sailors in Shairyn uniforms to watch the guard. Raiden was sure that if this did not get over soon, the knights and lion warriors who had walked into the tower would be over in seconds.

Inside were two knights with their backs to the front door as they watched the guard in case Mangus tried to escape. They were not ready for the door behind to bust open. Travis and John were the first followed by Raiden, Ariel, and Dick. Travis and John pulled out the daggers, jumping towards the knights. The knights tried to turn around quickly to see why the door was open or what the sounds were from, but they did not have a chance. The daggers pierced the knights' armor. The knights' armor offered no protection against the blue-glowing daggers, which sank into their backs. The knights stumbled forward, not yet dead but in severe pain, the sailors could see. Raiden and Ariel jumped forward, grabbing the left shoulder of the knights to hold them in place.

They thrust their swords into the knights with their blades, slicing through the front of the armor.

Lucifer saw the swords go through the knights by the front door, and the knights falling to the floor. Lucifer could tell this would not end well, moving into the shadows of the kitchen and grabbing his radio. "Bandits. Present, all knights engage." Once Lucifer was done, he looked and saw a door that led into the small yard behind the house. He leaped out of the house as more of the knights fell to the ground. Outside, to his left, was a gateway door that led to a path out into the city square. He opened the gate door and was out, waiting for the backup of knights and lion warriors to get to the house. Lucifer was confident that Mangus and the Bandits would soon be defeated.

As Mangus took down one of the last Knights in his house, he saw the duke in the dining room. The dining room was an open space with room. This all started with only one exit out into the kitchen. which luckily, one sailor was in front of. Mangus knew that the lion member who was not even a real duke could be dealt with now. As he moved forward, ready to kill, Raiden moved in front.

"Wait! We need him to find out what is going on." Mangus stepped back for a second, thinking, and then, with full strength from the adrenaline going through him, Mangus pushed Raiden to the side. Moving fast and swinging his fist at the lion's member. Mangus hit the lion's member with such power that the lion's member fell to the ground. As the member tried to get back up, Mangus kicked him in the face, and with that, he was out cold. Mangus signaled for some sailors to grab the member and bring him with them.

Mangus then ran to the chairs where his children were and cut the ropes that held them to the chairs. Both jumped off the chairs into the arms of their father with tears in their eyes. "We must go," Mangus told his children. The two sailors in disguise ran into the house. "We have to get out of here." They both said. Raiden looked and could see a giant group of knights and warriors coming out of the glass tower. Raiden looked around, not seeing any way to truly get out of the house.

"Follow us," Mangus told everyone. He and his children moved to a closet door. Mangus opened it. He moved his hand through the coats hanging and landed it on the wall. In just a second, a line of red light slid across under his hand. The wall slid out, and there was a stairway down. Mangus waved to his kids and everyone else to go down the stairs. Once Raiden, Ariel, the sailors, and the sailors carrying the unconscious lion's member were through. Mangus moved into the closet and through the door, then a few steps down the stairs, pushed a small button on the wall. The door he had opened slid back into place, and now there was not a trace of what had happened to Mangus, his family, and the group.

CHAPTER 40

It was outrageous to Lucifer that these knights did not even confront the bandits. From what the leading knights who stood right in front of him had explained, Bandits, Mangus, his family, and the duke had disappeared. There was no trace of where they went. When the warriors and knights entered the house, they found only a blood-covered floor and the dead bodies of the knights. They informed Lucifer that the Lions member was now missing, too. Lucifer knew that none of this was good. Where are they? That is all Lucifer could think of. He knew that if he waited much longer, Mangus could fight. Noon remained the scheduled time for both the execution and the Shairyn army's arrival at the Gateway. He did not need to give Mangus and the bandits a chance to stop them.

"Research the building. There must be a secret exit."

"Yes, sir." The leading knight said before turning around and heading out of the clan meeting room, followed by the other knights. Lucifer turned around, looking at the three representatives of the Lions, Serpent, and Hawks clans who sat at the table. The group was letting out the signs of how angry and worried they were about the situation. But it did not really matter too much. Once the army reached Gateway, Lucifer would eliminate the greedy families.

"We must stand down."

"Of course, the Hawks clan wants to be cowards." The Serpent clan member replied.

"Both of you shut up. It is too late to stand down. We must speed up the process of the Lions clan being in charge again." The lion's member shouted out. Both the representatives of the Serpent and Hawks clans stopped their argument.

"I can signal the army that they need to move in immediately." Lucifer pointed out. All three of the representatives said "good," at the same time, "What about Mangus?"

Even though it was a good question, it was not something Lucifer wanted to discuss at this moment. "Forget about him for now."

"How? If he finds help, he could cause some enormous problems."

"I get it, but my knights are currently rounding up warriors from the other clans." All three of the men looked surprised. Lucifer knew they hadn't expected him to take charge. "The clan leaders of the crows, tigers, shamrocks, eagles, bears, O'Brien, Murphy, McMackin, and smaller clans are all being held in the building's basement." From that news, all three were a little more at ease, but it still bothered them that knights were storming the city at night without team leaders from the lions, serpents, and hawks clans.

"You must prepare for the execution tomorrow morning." If the knights and soldiers arrived earlier this morning, then speeding up the display of the lions' control also made sense to Lucifer.

"At dawn tomorrow, you must return the items that were stolen from the train," Lucifer told the clan representatives, who all looked at each other with faces of anxiety. Speeding up the process would only make this harder for them. But they all understood the reason for what Lucifer was talking about. As he walked out of the room, Lucifer considered that success would earn him a higher rank. Plus, it would be nice if, when he could again be his true beast self, this event, killing off the peasant warriors who had no chance against him, were in his mind. Lucifer missed the battles he was once in, but to him, this was all worth it. Going from private to lieutenant so fast was crazy, but with the takeover of Gateway. Who knew what his reward would be?

Lucifer walked out of the tower, putting his hood up just in case someone in Gateway was awake already, and headed to the house. Lucifer walked through the broken front door. The knight in charge met him.

"Sir."

"Did you find anything?" Lucifer asked. He was getting frustrated in this whole situation. Even though he could tell that the knights had ripped this house apart. A group of Knights stood by a closet door.

"Yes, we have, sir." The knight walked over to the closet and showed Lucifer a hand scanner on the back wall of the closet. Now it was obvious to Lucifer that Mangus and the bandits had disappeared behind the door.

"Could you open it?" Lucifer asked.

"No, sir. The settings appear to be for the clan leader only. We have tried to shoot it open and just broke it open using one spear, but nothing has worked so far. We are waiting for your approval to use explosives."

"Do it," Lucifer commanded.

"Yes, Sir."

Two of the knights walked into the living room where the bodies were and picked up a box. They opened it up, and inside was an invasion explosive that could be stuck to any wall, door, or barrier that needed to be opened or out of the way and by remote set off from up to 500 ft away. All the knights left the house and gathered around supplies, putting on gas masks to protect themselves from the dust that was going to come out.

"3, 2,1," the knight said before hitting the button on the remote. A big bang went off, and you could hear parts of the walls crumble to the ground with smoke and dust blowing out the front door. They all waited a few seconds for the smoke to clear a little. The group of knights slowly walked up to the front door with automatic assault rifles, laser points, and scopes set ready to shoot at any movement in the building. The leading knight throws two explosive tear gas containers. Both go off with the contact to the floor.

The knights could hear nothing, and no one ran out of the building in pain, so they moved forward. The place was smoky, but it was still easy for the knights to see their way. Once they came to the closet. They determined that the closet, stairs, and doorway were destroyed. The leading knight came to the doorway, signaling two to take guard and the rest to follow him. They came to the doorway and saw stairs leading down into what the knight figures were, the tunnels under the city that they had used themself to get around the city without being noticed, and how they got into the city.

"Clear," the leading knight said as Lucifer walked in. The cloud of smoke and gas was out of the way. He came to where the leading knight and his followers stood. He looked and saw the stairs that the

Knights had uncovered.

"I need you and another squad, along with a K-9 soldier, to go down and find out where the group has gone."

"Yes, Sir."

The leader left the building, and the rest of the knights took guard on the stairs just in case someone returned. Lucifer was sure they would not find them because of all the tunnels and pathways under the city, but they had to at least try. Even with this chaos, the big show was going to happen, and this city would be the Dynasties by noon. Lucifer walked out of the building, hood up, towards the tower, where he would rest for a few minutes before it all fell into motion.

CHAPTER 41

The tunnels were dark and moist with brick walls. As Raiden walked in the tunnel, he could branch off, meaning that to Raiden, there were hundreds of separate ways to move through Gateway without being noticed. Mangus's children and the Sailors followed Raiden, Ariel, and Mangus to a large circular-shaped vault. With three other halls leading north, east, and west out of the room. A thin column stood in the middle of the room.

"Where are we?" asked Ariel.

"This is the emergency strategy room," Mangus answered while putting his hand on the Column. Just like the wall in the closet, a line slid under his hand. Once the line slid, everyone heard a peaceful woman's voice. "Hello, Master." The event puzzled and surprised everyone in the room.

"Iris, alert as many warriors as possible to meet here."

"Yes, master,"

"And put us into Alert 5."

"Yes, master." And with that, the entryways out of the large room had metal doors sliding together, followed by a loud click sound coming from every doorway. Then the walls lit up with images from cameras across the city, along with control of the gates. Mangus walked over to the North wall and pushed one brick into the wall. It took a bit of time, but then the voice returned.

"Emergency Alert master."

"Yes. "With that, Mangus turned to the biggest image and waited for a minute. But nothing happened.

"What is going on?" In a light voice, Raiden asked.

Before Mangus could answer, the voice returned. "I am disconnected from the dominant system."

"How?" Mangus asked.

Iris answered, "It looks like a member of the House of Lions used their connection into the system. From system analytics, it is the device used to open the doors of the car on the railroad mission.

For Raiden, it made no sense, but Raiden could tell that it was special to Mangus. Mangus's face revealed his redness. Without hesitation, he punched the image on the wall. You could hear his heavy breath. "Iris, how do we reconnect you to the full system?"

"The Security program used to disconnect me is unbreakable."

"BULLSHIT!"

Before Mangus punched the wall again, Raiden interrupted, "What about him?" pointing over towards the duke whom they had brought with them. He lay against the wall with the two sailors camouflaged as knights looking over him. Those words were exactly what Mangus needed to hear.

"Iris fridge." And with that, a small part of the south wall opened, letting out a fog of chilly air. Mangus grabs a metal jug. He unscrewed the lid to the container, walked over to the duke, then poured the whole jug onto the duke's head.

The duke woke up instantly from the severe chill and looked around with a puzzled face before realizing he was with Mangus, whom he was supposed to have killed earlier that night. Mangus bends over, grabbing the duke by the collar of his fancy outfit, lifting him up, and then slamming him against the brick wall.

Mangus then threw the duke across the room. "What has the house of scum done now?" he asked in a voice of anger. "House of Loin, you pathetic fool," and as the duke tried to get back up and fully stand. Mangus ran over and swung his foot right into the duke's gut. The duke dropped to the floor in pain.

Mangus knew that beating up a Lion member would change nothing. Even with Lions clan members being weak in a lot of ways, they could still be extremely loyal to their clan and take a good amount of pain in the clan's honor. However, this member did not seem to tolerate much pain, no matter the situation.

Mangus moved to pick up the duke again. He saw a cocky grin on the duke's face. With a second to think, the duke spat into Mangus' face. "I will tell you nothing."

"We will see about that," Mangus replied.

"Iris, table, and chair."

"Yes, Master." And in a few seconds, a blue-colored mist appeared by the column in the middle of the room, and magically, a metal table and chair came into view. No one could understand where it came from. On the table was a rope.

"Iris, I am impressed you know what I was doing," Mangus said.

"Yes, master, do you need anything else?"

"Not at the moment, Iris, see if you can find an old connection to the system," Mangus said.

"Yes, master."

Mangus then threw the duke towards the table and chair. The duke got up quicker than expected and ran towards Mangus, ready to swing, but before getting the chance, a block of the rock floor popped up about an inch right in front of his foot, tripping him. The duke slammed face-first right into the floor.

"Unnecessary, Iris," Mangus said.

"Sorry, Master." Mangus lifted the duke by his collar and then dragged him across the floor over to the chair. Mangus put the duke in the chair. Still dizzy from the collision with the floor, the duke didn't realize what was going on. Mangus quickly tied the duke to the chair, his right arm on the table. From the way he swung his hand before he tripped and the movements he did at the house, it was obvious that his right hand was his dominant hand.

The duke's mind became clear again. He remembered what was going on and tried to stand up and move his right hand, but Mangus's knife pierced right into his hand as he tried to move it. The duke screamed in pain.

"Now, what is going on?" Mangus asked.

The duke was in pain. Mangus could see tears running down his face, but he still replied in anger and resentment, "Fuck you."

Mangus pushed the knife in deeper with a small twist to help increase the sharp pain.

"You are losing your fingers if I ask again." Again the duke was replaying fuck you, but before he could finish the sentence pushed, he shoved the knife as far as possible. The duke screamed in pain again, with tears running down his face. "You will pay for this."

"We will see," Mangus answers. He looked over at Raiden with an easy-to-understand face. Without hesitation, Raiden pulled out and threw over his knife. Immediately not asking another question, Mangus slashed the knife into the duke's index and middle finger. Clearly slice them off the duke's hand. Again, screaming in pain, and then in a light voice, from loss of breath from the screaming and crying. "You win."

"Good. Now, what has your family done?"

"My grandfather made an agreement with the dynasty on their taking over Gateway." The duke answered.

"What agreement?" Mangus asked.

"We agreed we would take over Gateway and partner with the dynasty." Mangus's face was red with anger. "What the fuck, why?"

"My grandfather wants his power back. After you became clan leader, you lost all your power and dignity. To him, the dynasty would give him the right to rule as he deserves, the duke answered. It all made sense to Mangus that the Lions clan would do such things for power and money; the Lions clan's biggest problem was greed. It was disgusting to Mangus that they would dare even work with the dynasty after all the lives lost for the clans to win independence from the ruling of the Dynasty.

"What is the Dynasty's plan?" Mangus saw the signs that this was a question that the duke did not want to have answered. Before the duke answered, Mangus picked up the knife, rubbing the blood off the sleeve of his shirt, preparing to slice off some more fingers. The duke understood what was going to happen and answered the question.

"At the tower, my grandfather and family are to execute all the Clan leaders who stood up against the dignity of the Lions." The duke said. To Mangus, the Loins clan was no more a clan, just a gang of scum. "The Army of the dynasty will move at noon and finish its mission." To Mangus, that meant that they had time still, since the sun had not risen yet, and that it was not a full army in Gateway for now.

"How are they entering Gateway?" Mangus asked. Again, the duke held back on answering. Mangus just lifted his knife and set up to cut off another finger. The duke understood and answered, "The secret river opening."

Mangus knew exactly what he meant. That was the spot-on north part of the riverfront that was guarded by naval mines and chains to help block the entry if needed. It was the usual way for royalty, spies, and people from foreign countries to enter Gateway. With the knights controlling most of Gateway by now, it would be easy for the mines and chains to be turned off and the dynasty to move in.

Mangus had had enough of this spoiled brat. As he raised his head to see what Mangus's reaction was to his last words, Mangus swung his fist. Hitting the want-to-be duke in the cheek, a sucker punch, and knocking him out cold again. So many sucker punches guaranteed the duke a concussion.

Just as the man went out cold, Iris returned. "We have individuals approaching the north doorway."

"Show me."

In seconds on the wall, a picture of the individual is approaching. Mangus put on a smile. "Open it up."

"Yes, Master." Immediately, the guard door opened. A group entered the area. From Mangus's reaction and the outfits the individuals wore, it was easy to tell that it was some warriors who had escaped. It was a group of up to twenty warriors who had made it.

"Good to see you, Abban," Mangus announced.

"Good to see you too, Mangus," Abban replied, who was the leader of the group of warriors. Abban was a Scottish ancestor. His clan was one of the ready-for-battle at any time clans of the gateway.

"You ready to make history?" Abban continued to Mangus.

Immediately, they could hear a light sound. To Abban and Mangus, it was the notification bells of the city. But why did they think?

"Iris, what's going on?" Mangus asked.

The voice returned with an answer.

"Master, the Lions are notifying the citizens to gather at the tower by dawn."

"Can you stop it?"

"No, master, I am still not connected to the system."

"How can you fix that?" Mangus asked.

"To my knowledge, master, I need someone to upload my invasion virus directly into the guarded system." Mangus knew what that meant. Someone had to get to the Lions clan home and hook up the computer genesis from the Union, the neighboring nation, using a flash drive with the virus delta into the system through a USB port. This complete computer system they had now was still confusing sometimes to Mangus, but he trusted the Union with where it stood against the Dynasty and all the equipment it had supplied to Gateway in the last decade.

"Everyone!" Mangus yelled.

The entire group of people, from the warriors, sailors, Ariel, and Raider, stopped talking among each other and turned to see what

Mangus said, "We have a battle to start." Mangus continued, "I need all of you to help me and the clan warriors stop the dynasty from taking over Gateway." Mangus could notice some sailors were not completely open to this battle idea. "To whom is not my fellow warriors, I will pay you well." The sailors all smiled.

"Abban, and whoever else is here from your Clan, needs to get this into the Lions' computer system." Mangus put his hand on the column he stood by in the middle of the room. It scanned his hand and replied, "Omega Mangus." A small doorway slid open in the middle of the column, and there was the flash drive Mangus was talking about. Mangus picked up, walked over to Abban, and handed it over. Abban picked it up and signaled his fellow clan members to follow. Out of the fourteen warriors, six moved to follow Abban. "Who will help Abban?" Mangus asked the rest of the group. The two sailors dressed as guards and Ariel raised their hands. "Good, refill the weapons that you have and follow Abban," Mangus said, and at that same time, on the south wall, three giant closet doors opened. Inside, on the walls, were guns, bows, and all the bullets and arrows someone could ever ask for.

"Now, who will help me in the town square by the tower?" Mangus asked. The rest of the sailors, Raiden, and the rest of the warriors all knobbed yes before Mangus told everyone to go on a mission.

"Mangus, my friend Diego, and approximately seven more sailors could join," Raiden said.

To Mangus, that would help amazingly. "Good. Have them and two of my warriors meet at the city's tunnel entrance, just in case soldiers reach the entry tunnel before we restart the system."

"Where are they at?" Mangus asked Raiden.

"At a bakery by the docks of the river," Raiden replies. Mangus knew exactly what he meant. There was only one bakery in that part of town that would be open at this time of the morning.

"Iris, can you connect to Susan's Bakery?"

"Yes, Master, I can still connect to businesses." It was always surprising to Mangus how much Iris could hide and still do with the Lions locking her out of the main governmental system. In a few rings, the screen opened with Susan on video.

"Hello." She smiled as she said it.

"Good to see you. May I ask how the morning is going?" Mangus replies.

"Well, now, I was worried that we had already lost."

"Us Clan members never lose without a fight, you know that, Susan." Mangus pointed, and Susan smiled in agreement.

"Are there some warriors I may talk to?"

"Yes." She turned the camera over to Diego and Captain Pen.

"My Name is Mangus, if you don't remember." Diego knobbed and Captain Pen was a little surprised. He had never met the leader of the clans before.

"I need you to go here," a picture uploaded onto the screen. In seconds, Mangus could hear a printer going off in the background. Good old Iris, he thought. "To stop the dynasty from getting into Gateway." Mangus realized the captain was worried and a little confused. "It should be much; we should have defense up before the dynasty steps foot into Gateway, but we need to make sure. Are you willing to help?"

"Yes," Diego answers, but Captain Pen did not.

"Well, your fellow sailors here," Mangus turned, pointing over to the sailors in the room, "Have agreed to help for a good payment. Are you willing to do the same?"

It didn't even take a second, and Captain Pen replied, "Yes."

With the missions set, it was time to set off and stop the Lions and the dynasty.

With the warriors, sailors, and Raiden and his friends. Raiden felt they had a chance to win this battle, but only if things worked out for all three groups. "Let's go then," Mangus commanded. He turned to his son, who stood with Mangus's young daughter.

"You protect your sister and Iris at all costs. Do you understand?" His son nodded yes in excitement. This was going to be his son's first battle. Mangus knew staying here with Iris was the safety plan for his children. Mangus understood that this was going to be one of the greatest battles left in history, and no guarantee of who would survive and who would win. It was an all-or-nothing battle.

CHAPTER 42

Diego and the rest of the sailors from the dock reached the doorway. The door stood on the side of what just looked like an average house in Gateway, but it was not. It was a stairway inside to the tunnel that led straight to the secret entry to the city.

Diego touched the door. A screen lit up with a keyboard across it. Keyboards were not a usual thing you saw anywhere in the Shairyn Dynasty land, and understanding how to write was becoming rare. Thankfully, Diego's parents were scholars before the Dynasty rounded up intelligent people and forced them, for pay, to work as engineers, researchers, and doctors; protesting meant slavery and more menial labor.

Diego typed in the code deltaX2v19QHk99, the sound of a large lock unlocking; Diego heard. It was not too loud, but it was easy for Diego to tell that this was more sophisticated than one of the normal bank-safe locks. The door slid into the wall and was open. The lights turned on, flickering a little. And there was the stairway to the tunnel that Mangus had talked about. Diego and the sailors walked down the stairs. The tunnel had brick walls, going up ten feet. At the top of the wall, there was a curved top made of the same type of bricks.

They all could feel a moist, damp feeling, which they thought was because of the entry into the river. They walked down the tunnel, and at the end, there was an opening. Normally, five-foot-thick doors were used to shut the gateway, thus blocking floodwaters. At the entry, to the left, was the stream of water that led to a barred entry into the city. Diego figured that led to an acidelectrolyzed water disinfection machine that sanitized the water and created the city water for the people to use.

To the right, there was a walkway on the edge of the stream, only three feet above the stream. The walkway, made of bricks like the tunnel they had walked through, descended to a secret Gateway entrance where the Mud River entered the stream tunnel. Measuring about ten yards wide, the river flowed into a small stream. The walkway that led to the river was about fifteen feet wide, Diego thought, and it looked like it was thirty yards away from the entry. Close to the Entryway were three boats docking, with around twenty Knights getting off.

"You guys ready?" Diego asked. The sailors all knobbed yes but Diego could tell that they were nervous about the battle that was about to start. Diego quietly walked out onto the walkway. The Knights did not see him, so he signaled the sailors to wait. He moved down the walkway quietly, and once he was around ten yards away, one of the Knights who had gotten onto the walkway noticed him. Diego quickly threw one of the stun grenades he had.

The blast of blinding light and the intense, loud bang stunned the Knights. "Charge!" Diego yelled.

The Sailors took off running towards Diego. As they approached, Diego dropped his bag, which he carried next to him, and it took a second to unload, but he pulled out the heavy machine gun he had gotten at the gathering of weapons they had gone to before they took off on the mission to stop the train. Just as the Knight became more stable and was about ready to respond to what was going on, Diego opened fire with the heavy machine gun, taking down five of the Knights immediately.

The Knights behind the front Knight, who had taken the machine gun fire, flare up their plasma shields. The Shields could barely block the bullets, but Diego could tell that the shields would last longer than the ammunition belt that Diego had. Thankfully, the Knights had to hold up their shield and could not fire back at Diego, who flooded the walkway with bullets. Just as Diego was running out of bullets, the sailors got into battle position. The first two kneeled with their rear knee on the ground and their other knee in position to support the elbow of the forward arm. The gun was in position with the receiver end set into their shoulders. Three other sailors stood behind them, one armed with a semi-automatic rifle and the other two with bows. They must have had the experience of battle, which was excellent for Diego.

Using their bows, two archers shot two arrows at the knights with their shields raised. The Arrows were like what the Arrows used to electrocute people in battle. Splitting the arrow tips created four objects. The objects landed on the Knights' shields and automatically let out a wave of electricity that neutralized the shields. But with how long the shields had been up, and how many more of the knights could dock and get off the boats. There was an automatic backfire. One knight threw a fast-obscuring grenade. Blasting thick fog in front of Diego and the sailors.

The knights returned fire immediately, hitting one sailor with the bows. The attack hit one sailor in the shoulder, knocking him to the brick floor, and he dropped his bow into the stream. His injury meant he could only use his handgun. The other sailor received several blows to the chest, causing him to fall dead to the floor. He dropped his bow, and blood covered the walkway.

Diego knew this would not end well if they stayed in position. "Retreat!" Diego commanded and hoped all four of the sailors heard him. They all retreated into the tunnel they used to get to the entryway.

To Diego, this was not looking good. He took his only shockwave grenade and turned his head around the corner to see how close the knights were. They were moving slowly but forward with their weapons ready to fire. Diego took the Shockwave, throwing it down the walkway. Shockwaves were anti-tank grenades, making Diego feel as if he did as he wished.

The grenade landed on the walkway, barely in front of the leading knights. On the impact of hitting the floor, it exploded. The shockwave was so powerful that it shook the walls that Diego and the sailors were standing by. Diego looked around the corner again, and the grenade did as he wanted it to, taking out a handful of knights and breaking down and crumbling part of the walkway. Diego felt the walkway crumble, and now the Knights, thinking he might have more similar grenades, would hold back for the moment. But Diego knew they would still move forward at some point. Diego understood the sailors and knew he'd be in trouble when they moved.

CHAPTER 43

The light of the morning sun was slowly brightening the sky. Ariel knew they only had a small amount of time to finish this mission. All she had to do was get the flash drive into the wall USB slot, and that was it. The problem was that at just the doorway to the house of the Lions were over ten warriors and a few dynasty knights. She understood they had to wait for a little longer, hoping the group would move on.

Just as Ariel had thought, the leading Lions member and old man, in his late sixties, walked out and down the stairs with his sons and grandchildren following him. They were all grown men from forty years old to in their early twenties. A few looked like teenagers. Knights preceded and followed a large group of men and a few women.

It took Ariel a moment before she realized it was some members who were at the meeting, sitting around the table, when they had first arrived in Gateway a week ago. The group walked over to a group of vehicles. One was obviously a prisoner bus, the other four were what Ariel knew from the old tales, SUV. They loaded the prisoners onto the bus, with a few knights following in the four SUVs. The vehicle took off down the street, vanishing a few blocks down. Leaving behind only five warriors.

Ariel, Abban, the two sailors, and the six warriors did not know how many lion warriors were in the house, but it was time for them to move forward. Abban signaled the warriors to attack. Four of the six warriors ran out, and behind them were the two warriors who took their bows shooting pairs of arrows into the sky at an arch making it so that they went over the charging warriors and struck into Lion warriors or land near the five lion warriors outside of the entryway to the lion's den. The lion warriors did not see what was coming. The two Archers reached their goal with a pair of arrows. Each archer had at least one of the two arrows they shot, landing on one lion warrior each.

One landed on the back of one warrior at an angle. The warrior's reaction to collapse after impact, most likely meaning the arrow hitting directly into the warrior's spine at full force. Paralyzing him for the rest of the battle and for the rest of his life from this point. The other arrow hit another warrior in the back calf of his left leg. The warrior screamed in pain and fell to the ground. With two warriors collapsing to the ground by the front of the building, the last three warriors immediately knew they were under attack. The lion's warriors charged towards Ariel, Abban, the sailors, and the thunder warriors.

The sailors, Abban and Ariel, knew they had to get past the lion's men and into the house. Ariel figured that once they killed the last three lion men, the rest of the thunder warriors could join them inside the lions' den. The four of them slipped by the battle, seeing two lone warriors lying dead on the ground, meaning only one still stood. One thunder warrior suffered an injury, but it didn't stop him from fighting.

At the front door, Ariel could hear the marching footsteps of lion warriors charging towards the door. Ariel signaled Abban and the sailors about the lion's warriors coming towards the door. All four moved quickly into position. The two sailors got on the left side of the doorway with their backs against the wall. Ariel and Abban did the same. Ariel saw the last lion warrior fighting the thunder warriors fall to the ground. She whistled to get the warriors' attention and knobbed her head to the right, towards the door. Warning the thunder warriors that lions were coming. The two archers understood and took the front position, setting up aim.

The lion's warriors busted through the front door, in pairs, but spreading into four once they were out of the door. It was the perfect setup for the archers. The first arch shot his first arrow and, like Ariel had thought, it split into four pieces. Three of the four pieces land on three different lion warriors. The fourth piece ricocheted off the other warrior's shoulder. Just as Ariel had expected, the three pieces that landed on the lion's warriors let out a burst of electricity, shocking the three warriors. The one that missed and landed on the ground let out a burst of electric sparks. The second archer shot a glowing blue tip arrow penetrating the chest armor of the fourth warrior, splitting into the warrior's flesh, and cutting his superior vena cava, causing instant death. Blood poured past his front armor as he landed on the ground.

The thunder warriors put up their plasma shields after taking out the first line of lion warriors. The lion warriors slowed down into a slow but steady charge, with a few blue arrows ricocheting off the shields. This means to Ariel that the dynasty must have upgraded the shields and weaponry of the lion's warriors as part of the agreement between the lions and the dynasty. A few seconds later, the full group of ten lion warriors left the building and passed Ariel, Abban, and the sailors. Ariel and Abban sneaked into the building. Ariel turned her head, looking at the two sailors in lion warriors' outfits, pointing her index finger at the warriors behind them. They understood that each sailor had removed a small metal sphere from the warrior's belt. They each squeezed the spheres. One glowed with a blue light and the other glowed with a red light. One sailor rolled out the blue sphere on the ground towards the group of lion warriors, heading towards the thunder warriors in front of the building. The sailor quickly shut the front door. Seconds later, they heard an explosion go off, killing and injuring who knew how many lion warriors. A few seconds after the explosion, the other sailor barely opened the door, and this time, rolling out the red glowing sphere. It went off with a flash of light and a burst of ear-splitting noise. It stunned the lion's warriors, who were just getting up and standing after the first explosion. They could hear the thunder warriors take advantage of the flash, charging into battle.

Ariel signaled the sailors to take guard of the front door to prevent any lion warriors from returning to the building. Ariel and Abban looked around the front room. It was most likely that the family members, women, children, and men who did not know how to fight were in the basement bunker. Ariel knew they had a limited amount of time before more warriors would arrive because of communication connections that the family members had in the basement. She could tell this was a big house with a large entryway openly connected to the living room. Both Ariel and Abban saw the open stairs to the second floor leading to the bedrooms of the house. A single door was located under the stairs that led to the upper floor. Ariel believed it led to a kitchen.

The living room was full of expensive, to most people unaffordable, furniture and ancient artwork. No one knew, but besides her obsession with cats, the ancient artwork fascinated Ariel. She had learned about artwork from some of the elderly from her hometown, Land City, mostly known as Cedar Falls, to the elderly. There were libraries of ancient books about artwork, published even before the final war, which by itself was over two millennia ago.

She recognized the George Washington portrait, the Declaration of Independence paintings, and one of her favorite American Gothic paintings. These paintings were worth thousands or millions of gold. Paintings like these were what she heard were only in places like Nova. Ariel could remember the elderly talking about a place once called America, which was one of the big countries involved in the Final War. Even the elderly had little knowledge of the causes, events, or battles of the final war. All they knew was it had destroyed most of the world. And it destroyed the ancient cities that Raiden, Diego, and she went metal hunting in, like the windy city.

Ariel signaled Abban to go into the living room, and she said she would check out any other room connected to it. She went to the doorway under the stairs. Once she opened the door, it was, as she expected, a doorway to a kitchen. It was a giant kitchen compared to the kitchen that Ariel had back in Sand Town and the tiny one she lived with as a child in Land City.

There were multiple stoves, grills, and fresh water sinks, it looked like. It was a beautiful kitchen, much fancier than the type in Sand or any in the land of the Shairyn dynasty besides Nova itself. She could tell that the stoves were not wooden, and wood was rare in the dynasty, and they did not look like coal. The Shairyn dynasty forbade the use of coal. The ancients said that coal and a dark-colored liquid they called black gold owed their existence to the dry, hot, desert-like weather of the flatlands and the near-uninhabitability of the southwest.

To Ariel's right was a door, mostly leading into the room Abban was exploring. But at the end of the room was a swinging double doorway. Ariel walked over with her dagger in one hand and her handgun in the other. At first, as she got closer, she heard nothing. The closer she got, the more she could hear heavy breathing and light whimpering like a cry. She opened the door, ready for action if needed. Inside were two old ladies, the experts in the kitchen, and a dozen junior staff. The youngest staff were just children and teenagers, with two other grown adults who were assistant managers, Ariel thought. Ariel pointed at them and then waved her finger at the doorway. The group knew exactly what Ariel meant and left. They all slowly and quietly moved past Ariel. With the Kitchen experts last, they whispered to Ariel, Thank you. Ariel believed the staff's treatment closely resembled slavery, a consequence of the lion's clan members' self-centeredness and ignorance. To them, anybody who was not part of the family or their colleague families was trash and nothing else, according to what Ariel had picked up from what Mangus and his warriors had said back in the emergency headquarters.

Ariel looked around. The room that the kitchen staff had hidden in was an enormous pantry closet. Full of canned food, bakery products, and some liquor bottles, at the end of the closet was the doorway to what Ariel figured was a cooler, and then further in, a freezer. She thought their wealth spoiled these rich backstabbers and wished she had similar things back home in Sand Town. She wondered how good the food was from the cooler and freezer. The baked goods and other foods she could smell on the shelves of the pantry smelled delicious, almost unbelievable. If only she could try some, she thought to herself. It had been a year since she was home and had freshly baked goods. Even just a homemade meal. But she had to get going. She was on a mission and did not have time to stand around. She spun around and walked over to the door leading into the room Abban was in.

She opened it and walked through the doorway. Once she was in, she saw what the room was. A dining room, with a giant oak table and chairs. It looked beautiful. The oak looked natural with a clear varnish over it. Ariel figured this was the dining set that came from the northern part of the dynasty, past Nova, into the great forest. Or somewhere southeast in the land where the Union had blocked off all travel and trade. At the end of the table, by the doorway leading out of the dining room, stood Abban.

Abban was looking down the hall that passed the exit to the dining room. Right across from him on the other side of the hall was a double door made of wood and metal. From Ariel's knowledge, it looked like doors, if locked, you could not open with just a kick. Somehow, it needed to be unlocked. Ariel moved over next to Abban. "Is it locked?"

Abban knobbed yes. "How are we going to open it?" Ariel asked.

"Don't worry, I've got it," Abban replied. He then moved over and took out a small pouch. It was a thief unlocking kit. That was something she was not expecting. Abban, a thief? She asked herself. He opened the pouch and took out a few small tools that Ariel had not seen before. He took the tools and messed around with the keyhole. It took a few minutes, and then she heard a click.

Abban looked back at Ariel, smiling, and said that it was open now.

CHAPTER 44

Ariel and Abban slowly opened the door, less than half an inch, to see if they could hear anything. They heard mumbling in the background, but could not tell what was going on. Ariel pushed it open a little, and thankfully, it made no extra sound. She looked around the door to see the room better. At just a glimpse, Ariel could tell that it was a two-story room that had a library and a half office. The library part had a bookshelf two stories tall up to the ceiling of the room, with a small ladder leading up to the top of the shelves. This allowed access to all the books on the shelves. Wheels on its bottom connected the ladder to rails running across all the shelves, making every book in the library accessible. The Shelves looked like they were full of ancient books made long ago.

From the glimpse, she could barely see past the door itself, but she could make out an office area with a large wooden desk with two chairs in front and a big, cuffed, professional business-looking chair behind it. She could see a little on the side of her, and it was a leather couch. Standing in front of the room by the desk were what Ariel bet were Delta Defense Knights. Instead of a basic bulletproof vest, jeans, a utility belt with ammo, and a basic backpack with supplies in it. The Defense Knights had metal-looking armor across their bodies, covering most of it with black clothing under it. They had assault rifles hanging from their shoulders, but also what looked like spears in their hands. Ariel believed the spears' full length had value beyond their spearheads.

Ariel looked at Abban, waving at him to come to her. Abban moved forward with his weapon ready for attack. The weapon differed from something she had seen before. It was like the symbol of the house of thunder, a warhammer. But it was different. It had what looked like a little blue glow to it. She pointed at it as Abban got close. Abban just whispered, "You'll see."

Ariel pointed to the back of the leather couch. Knowing what she meant, Abban quietly but quickly moved and got behind the leather couch. He had to kneel and duck to stay hidden. The couch was tall and wide, but Abban was a very tall and muscular man. Ariel followed Abban's footsteps and got behind the couch. Ariel shot her head up quickly to get a better look at the situation.

She pointed four fingers at Abban, pointing out that there were four Delta Knights. Then she showed two fingers for the possibility of lions, family members, or just civilians. Ariel then signaled Abban to go left, and she would go right. She got into position and, with precise action, Ariel's bow was up and aiming. In milliseconds, there was an arrow speeding up in silence. Abban followed with his Warhammer. Abban with a thick leather rope with small metal symbols at the end connected to the Warhammer. He threw the Warhammer straight at one of the Delta Knights. At first, it was like a normal Warhammer with its weight; it would head to the ground. But the light blue light that Ariel had noticed earlier was bright, and it was less than a microsecond. The lights flared up throughout the design on the Warhammer flashed, putting it into unbelievable momentum; it was like a blur of blue light. The Warhammer slammed into a Delta knight with such force that the knight flew back fifteen feet, hitting the bookcase. Knocking books off the shelf that landed on top of the knight. The knight would have to recover before he could join the fight, Ariel thought. Then she saw Abban squeeze his fist for a second, and the Warhammer he had thrown across lifted off the floor at the same speed it had when thrown. It came back, landing right in Abban's hand.

This all blew Ariel's mind, but she did not pay any attention to the arrows she shot that split into the four pieces which landed on three of the Delta Knights. The flare of electricity went off with just sparkles on the chest of the knights. It startled Ariel, reminding her she was right. Only blue-tipped arrows had the chance of piercing the Delta's armor.

The delta knight's plasma shields lit up, coming from a circle on the top of the armor on their left forearm. All three of the standing Delta Knights squeezed the shafts of their spears, flashing into a red glare at the tip of the spears. Ariel had six tip arrows, but she was not sure if the arrows could penetrate the plasma shields. She looked over at Abban. Abban took the flash drive he had in his pocket and threw it over to Ariel. Ariel caught it and put it into her pocket. She knew she had to get to the computer, where the two lions members were.

She looked around, spotted the Delta Knight the Warhammer had first struck, and shot it with a blue-tipped arrow. The arrow's glowing tip sliced through the armor effortlessly, just as Ariel predicted. The Delta knight fell to the ground. It was time for Ariel to get to the desk. Abban occupied the Delta. To Ariel and the Delta knights, Abban was more of a problem for them than she was.

CHAPTER 45

With Ariel now set to take care of the flash drive and the Delta knights determined to take him down, Abban lifted his Warhammer towards the ceiling straight above him, with only a few lights in the room altogether and three on right now. All the lights sparkled and glittered, followed by a flash of light and a surge of electricity connecting the lights and the Warhammer. All the light socket bulbs popped.

The surge of electricity connected to the war hammer shone in a bright blue; Abban swung the Warhammer down, pointing it straight at one of the delta knights with their shield up. The Warhammer let out a shock wave of power exactly like a lightning bolt, slamming into the Delta Knight plasma shield, which was standing in the middle of the three with other smaller bolts ricocheting off.

The middle Delta knight's shield was no match for the original bolt, which went through it effortlessly and into the chest of the Delta warrior. Electricity jolted his body, frying all his nerves. The delta knight collapsed to the floor of the room with a smolder coming from the delta knight's dead body.

Smaller bolts ricocheted, striking the shields of the two other knights, causing the shields to flicker. Abban concluded that a few more Warhammer hits would break the weakened shields, resulting in a proper battle. The bigger of the two knights charged forward towards Abban with his shield straight in front of him and the glowing red spear tip aimed right at Abban. The other Delta Knight waited behind to see what Abban's next move was.

Abban took his Warhammer and threw it into the Delta knight's shield. With a force, the delta knight slid back a few feet. Although it flickered again, the shield didn't break. Abban knew it was going to take more than just a hit from the Warhammer to neutralize the shields. Abban squeezed his hands again, and the Warhammer quickly returned to his grip.

The front knight charged forward, and the knight in the back did the same. Abban took the Warhammer, lifting it straight up again, swirling it in a small circle while holding it, and then with firmness and speed he slammed the head of the Warhammer into the floor like he was hitting a nail. The Warhammer let out a bright flash. The force of the Warhammer impact created a ripple across the floor, lifting the tiles and leaving a crack in the cement. With the dominant force of the rippled wave hitting the Delta knights, knocking them off the ground and back into the wall. Just the first knight hit, but this time with more force. The rippling wave even shook the furniture and desk.

The delta knights were stunned by the force they had just been hit by. Abban stood up and threw the Warhammer at one of the Delta knights, who was just getting up. The Warhammer hit the delta knight right in the middle of the helmet he was wearing. The helmet broke into pieces, and the Warhammer smashed into the delta knight's head, splitting into pieces that splattered all around the bookshelves and even on the other delta knights' armor. Abban ran forward, then jumped, slamming into the gut of the delta knight, pushing all the air out of his lungs.

The delta knight gasped for air, but Abban gave him no second to recover. Abban stood up, having the delta knight fall to his knees. Abban grabbed the top of the knight's helmet, shoving it forward as he quickly slammed his knee into the face of the delta knight. The front part of the helmet burst into pieces, and Abban's knee impacted the face of the delta knight. The delta knight's head wiggled. Abban let go of the back of the delta knight's helmet, and the delta fell to the floor.

Blood was oozing from his nose and cuts from his face, but he was barely awake, still trying to move an arm or leg. Abban took his right foot, with great might, kicked his foot into the face of the delta knight, knocking him out cold and with a concussion or serious brain damage.

CHAPTER 46

Ariel felt the chaos of Abban's battle going on and even felt the wave of force from Abban slamming his Warhammer to the floor. She had to finish the task. She had gotten to the desk and inserted the flash drive into the USB port, but nothing was happening. Ariel looked over from the chair she was sitting in and looked at the two lion members.

"You failed." One lion member shouted out. With no time to waste, Ariel took one of her daggers and threw it right into the leg of the lion's member, who had responded. The member burst into tears of pain, showing the fear in his eyes. Ariel took another dagger and looked at the other lion member. The other member shouted in fear, "I will help! I will help! Do not hurt me!" The other dynasty member said. The one in pain looked at the one who had surrendered with a frown, but was in such pain that he could not say anything, just tears of pain.

Ariel pushed the Enter button on the keyboard. The screen lit up. Ariel had never really used a computer much. Her father had shown her how to work with one when she was a young teenager back in Cedar Falls, but it had been a long time since she had messed with one since. The monitor screen showed a small rectangle, a vertical line marking its end.

"Ok. What is the password?" Ariel asked.

"The password is 6z75AbC2080#XY%99." The lion's member said to Ariel. To Ariel, that was a complicated password, but one of the best passwords that Ariel had ever heard. She typed it in, then pushed the Enter button the second the screen came on. It only took a few seconds, and then a square came in the middle of the screen.

Ariel heard a slam into the wall, hundreds of books falling off the shelves and landing on the ground. She turned her head to see what was happening and saw Abban finishing the fight and beating the last delta knight on the ground. She turned back to see the screen. On the front was the square that said delete. Rows of files were flowing through the box and vanishing at the end. What was going on? She thought. "What did you do?' the lion's member who had said the password grinned in an evil smile. You're fucked now." And without hesitation, Ariel took the other dagger she had and threw it, landing right in the left eye of the lion's member. Blood burst out and flooded down his face. The man screamed in pain, then fell backward, slamming into the floor, with blood flooding the floor. The other member had a knife in his leg. Went into shock. Even if he was happy with what his family member had done, he was now terrified that his life was over. Ariel took the last of her spare daggers and threw them into that loon's member's crotch.

The member screamed in torture. Ariel just smiled down at him. "You're welcome." Ariel looked up at Abban, who had finished with the delta knights.

"You get it?" Abban asked.

"I think so." She replied.

Abban asked no more questions. "Let's go help the others." He said. Ariel knobbed yes. They left the room through the door they entered through. Even in the dining room, Ariel still heard the lion's member crying in pain. She just grinned with a little joy. They entered the living room, and there stood the sailors.

"What was all of that about?" one sailor asked with a puzzled look on his face.

"Nothing, just a good battle," Abban answered.

"Ok, I guess." The sailor answered.

"Let's see if they need us outside." The sailors opened the front door, ready for more battle, but once the door was open, there stood the group of thunder warriors and the bodies of the lion's warriors. Ariel saw the lion's warriors who were killed by the grenade. She, some of her ally warriors, had died too. She saw the frontline lion warriors who died at the beginning of the battle.. Five of the six warriors stood guarding three lion warriors who were on their knees, preparing to die. They had won that battle, but now all she could do was hope that the virus was doing its job.

CHAPTER 47

The jail cells were small, but there were so many that all the captured warriors still fit in all the cells. This giant room was far into the basement of the Glass Tower. It was a room made of cement block walls with fluorescent lights on the ceiling. It was a little moist down there. Just on the other side of the jail cell walls were the pipes of water that went to the Glass Tower.

The warriors could still hear the crowd of people gathering in the town square. Most wondered what was going on. They knew that the Lions clan was doing something, but they did not fully know what. Most stood frustrated that they did not get the chance to fight the traitors who had rounded them up. They could all tell that they were angry at this whole situation.

Three lion warriors stood guard on the outside of the cells, blocking the doorway out of the basement with their rifles ready to fire. The warriors still could not think of any way for them to get out of the cells and attack these pathetic clan members.

A sound went off on the other side of the door to the jail cell room. At first, the lion's warriors did not care. It was just the normal sound of the basement activities of rats, they believed. But only a few seconds later, another sound went off. This time, it sounded like gunfire. All three lifted their rifles, ready to fire. They slowly moved and unlocked the door. One warrior kneeled into battle position. The warrior then hand signaled the other two to go out and see what was going on. The two warriors moved up and were ready for battle. Once the two warriors were out and heading down the hall to see what was going on, the third warrior followed them.

Instantly, as the warriors left the room, the doorway to each jail cell clicked open, unlocking, and the door to the room with jail cells shut with a heavy-sounding lock going into position. The warriors knew battle was imminent, but the events confused them.

The Voice of Iris turned on and said, "Time for battle, fellow warriors." They all knew what was going on now. Down at the end of the hall of the jail cells was the locked safe room where their weapons were; they all heard a large lock opening. They all smiled, feeling the thrill. It was time for battle.

"Get to the town square as soon as possible. Mangus is preparing for battle and will need all of your might." They went to the safe room and gathered their equipment. They got the armory, loaded the guns, and had their swords and axes out for battle.

"This is a surprise attack on lion warriors, their allies, and dynasty knights," Iris instructed. The warriors knew what to do. Most found hoods and robes, putting them over their armor to help hide themselves. Some did not get the chance to disguise themselves and knew they had to stay out of sight until the clan leader signaled them to charge into battle. After arming themselves, the warriors unlocked the door. Two of the warriors hid by the door as the lion's warriors burst in. The lion warriors could not open fire. The warriors standing by the doorway jammed their sword blades into the front of the two lion warriors. The lion warriors fell to the floor, bleeding. The third warrior stood back ready to open fire but one of the warrior from the crowd, in a flash threw three javelin knives at him, one landing in his face and the other two piercing through his armory into his chest, right into his heart and his superior vena cave spilling out blood like a river. He fell to the floor next to the other two traitors. The crowd of warriors cheered in gratitude that the battle had now begun.

CHAPTER 48

Raiden and Magnus walked out into the crowd of people as they gathered around in the town square. It was early morning, with no one expecting something this early. It was thousands of the citizens of Gateway. Mostly women, children, the elderly, and businesspeople. There was a wooden stage setup, which must have been under construction in the early hours of the morning. With multiple logs of wood around three feet tall, standing on the flat end in the middle of the stage. Raiden had seen this before in multiple little towns. It reminded him of when the dynasty was punishing the people in charge of the town for not listening, not spoiling them, or sometimes just because they could.

Raiden looked back at the group of sailors and warriors hidden in the back of the crowd wearing cloaks. Raiden was not sure why, but Magnus gave the order to his warriors to wait, and the sailors followed in the warrior's footsteps.

It took a while before most citizens of Gateway had gathered in the town square. They all looked puzzled about what was going on. A drum started beating, and Viking flutes were going off. As the old man leader of the lion's clan, Raiden recognized the man; he was the one who'd been angry with Mangus for allowing Raiden and his friends to take part in the train mission. The old man walked up the stairs to the stage. The flutes and drums hushed, and the bagpipes played Amazing Grace—a song, Raiden understood, usually reserved for Scottish rituals, according to some warriors Raiden talked to on the train mission.

Awaiting the music's end, the old man walked onstage before speaking.

"My fellow members of Gateway. We are here to honor our new leaders and punish the traitors who fought against us." As he finished, lion warriors walked a group of clan leaders onto the stage. Followed by the younger members of the lion's clan, the leaders of the serpent's and hawk's clans. The leaders all stood by the old man.

"I am Charles of the lion's Clan, and this is my fellow leader, Blake of the serpents, and Alvin of the hawks. We together will help Gateway thrive." Charles hand signaled his warriors to bring forward three of the clan leaders. They walked them up front to the wooden stubs. A headsman followed with a hood, a black mask, and his execution axe. The headsman positioned the men with their chins on the wood stubs and their hands cuffed behind their backs.

"Today, we punish those who try to hold back Gateway from thriving." Charles turned his head and knobbed at the headsman. The Headman knobbed back and walked over in to position by the first wood stub. Raiden knew what would happen and wanted to step forward, but knew it would not help the situation. There was enormous fear in the eyes of the clan leader that the headsman stood by. Once in position, Charles hand signaled the headman to do his job. With a quick flash, he lifted the execution axe, swung it, and sliced it through the neck of the clan leader. Blood splattered across the stage as the head fell off. The rest of the clan leaders were in position to be next and had eyes full of fear as they looked into the crowd.

"Now we have more people to punish for their actions against Gateway, but we will give the coward Mangus the chance to come forward, and we will spare the rest, and only kick them out and forbid them from returning to Gateway," Charles said. Raiden knew it was a lie. Charles, just like any other dictator figure, would still execute them all. Raiden heard a noise behind him. As Mangus walked by, he gave Raiden and the rest of the warriors a hand, signaling to stay for the moment. Raiden was a little surprised by Mangus's action, but knew that Mangus had to do something. Raiden watched as Mangus walked forward through the crowd, stepping in front and dropping his hood.

A group of lion warriors marches forward, meeting Mangus. They took his weapons and walked him onto the stage. Charles and the other two leaders grinned that they now had Mangus and could execute him, too. Raiden stood, wondering what they were going to do now. Charles walked over, meeting Mangus as he came onto the stage, grinning and pointing at the warriors to move Mangus into position to be beheaded like the other clan leader was. Charles walked back to the center of the stage. "Now we want the chaos-causing bandits to show themselves," Charles shouted out, looking around, but Raiden did nothing. He knew what was going to happen and if they were going to free Mangus and the city itself, his surrender would not help at all.

Charles turned around and waved at the lion warriors behind him. Two of them left the stage. The crowd started whispering, and businesspeople shouted out: Traitor. Moments later, the entire crowd was chanting Traitor. "QUIET YOU PEASANTS!" Charles shouted out. Immediately, almost twelve Shairyn knights appeared on the outskirts of the crowd with their guns up, ready to fire at the people who shouted out "traitor". The knights gunned down the businesspeople after only a few words. The businesspeople fell to the ground dead with bullet holes in their heads and hearts.

The crowd gasped and was afraid of what was going on. Raiden knew that something had to happen soon. But in horror, the two warriors who left the stage returned with Raiden's niece, Jessica. Followed by more knights and the man who fit the description of the man called Lucifer, who the people of Sand Town called the killer of Raiden's family. Raiden felt an anger build. He could taste revenge, but knew he had to save Jessica first. Raiden looked back at Jessica and could tell Jessica was angry and ready to fight, but he could also sense the fear.

With an evil grin, "Will the Chaos-causing bandits now come forward?" One warrior who walked with Jessica took his combat knife and pressed it against her neck in a position to just slice it and cause instant death. "You have one last chance. Come forward or she dies." The warrior pressed the knife more against her skin, and Raiden could see a drip of blood coming off her throat. Without even a thought, Raiden pulled his hood back and put his hands up. Charles noticed him immediately behind the crowd. The Four Knights left the stage and met Raiden halfway. They took his weapons and walked him onto the stage with assault rifles aimed at him and one touching his back. The Knights put him in a position to behead. "Now I will clean the city of its filth." Charles looked at the headman. The headsman got into position with an axe, ready to swing it down onto Mangus's neck. But just seconds before he could get into motion, there was a roaring explosion sound, Startling everyone in the crowd and on the stage.

CHAPTER 49

The roaring sound started repeating itself. Mangus knew that Raiden's friends and his fellow warriors had followed his orders. With all the sound, Charles was not paying attention, nor were his warriors or the headsman. The knights standing around him did not pay any attention to Mangus. Mangus jumped up and turned around in a flash, grabbing the cheeks of one of the knights' masks. Mangus moved his arms around, crisscross, while holding the knight's head and snapping the knight's neck. As the knight fell to the floor of the stage, Mangus grabbed his assault rifle. Before the other Knights had a moment to react, Mangus fired on them with the assault rifle, screaming "ATTACK!"

In sequence with the order, the other warriors and sailors went into battle. Dropping their cloaks and other camouflage. The sailors had orders to attack warriors or knights outside of the crowd to free the people. The warrior's orders were to storm the stage and take down as many lion warriors as possible. Mangus and the warriors realized they were outnumbered and would probably lose the battle without reinforcements, particularly if more knights appeared.

Mangus turned to his left, shooting the headsman standing next to Raiden. The man fell, and Raiden grabbed his axe and swung as he charged towards the two lion warriors, taking them down in a single blow. Mangus knew this was going to be a good fight. As the lion family headed off stage, more warriors of the lion's clan blocked Mangus's path to confront Charles. Mangus could tell with his warriors charging towards the stage that Charles and his family were stuck on stage. He just had to get through the row of lion warriors. Thunder warriors got into a battle with the knights and the lion warriors at the edge of the stage. It was up to Raiden and Mangus to fight who was on stage and to get to the traitors.

Mangus looked around and could tell that some sailors had already fallen but had taken out over half of the knights surrounding the people. Making it so that the citizens could escape. He saw a few teenage boys and a businessperson or two join the fight with the sailors, but he and his fellow warriors faced a three-to-one disadvantage. Raiden had grabbed a gun from a fallen lion warrior and was setting fire toward a group of hawk warriors and Shairyn knights. The warriors did not have protection from bullets, but some knights did. The warriors hid behind the knights, and the group moved forward. Mangus knew he was going to have to be in the front and take out the knights with shields who were protecting the traitors.

CHAPTER 50

Raiden was out of ammo, with only a handful of knights down before the rest had their shields up. They were ready to open fire on Mangus and him. The two did not have anywhere they could hide on the stage. This was over for them in Raiden's mind.

Surprisingly, they heard more noise out where the crowds were. Raiden looked, and more warriors were charging toward the stage. Iris must have freed the warriors. Now the enemy appeared outnumbered. With that noise, half of the group of warriors and a few of the knights charging Raiden and Mangus turned and went offstage to stop the crowd of new warriors. Raiden could still hear the naval mines going off in the muddy river. Taking down the reinforcement for the knights that were here. But still with no shields or ammo, He wouldn't be around to see the end of this great battle or to see his niece again, Raiden thought.

Raiden watched as an arrow struck one shoulder of the front knights with the shields. It landed on the knight's arm and burst into a blue cloud surrounding all the Knights and warriors. Raiden saw the faces of some warriors as their faces froze into an ice-colored blue. It was one arrow that Ariel loved. Raiden looked out, and on the outskirts of the town square were Ariel and Abban, with more charging warriors behind them. Raiden saw Abban throw something at the warriors. On stage, the object flew into one warrior at an unimaginable speed. It stunted Raiden on how strong that object was. Only seconds after impact, they were up in the air. It was a Warhammer, and it flew back into the grips of Abban. More arrows landed on the warriors. Multiple ally warriors had died, and there were still plenty of lions and knights fighting, but that was when, off to the edge, a large crowd of warriors started charging into the battle. The sound of metal clanking together, and gunshots as the battle went on. There was a level of dead bodies on the ground of the town square. But it was slowly ending where it was more ally warriors than knights and traitor warriors. After another couple of warriors and knights fell, the lion, serpent, and hawk warriors lowered their weapons and raised their hands to surrender. They knew they had lost the battle.

The faces of the traitor clans were fearful now. Charles was angry that he had lost and that his men were cowards now. Knowing they would be executed as traitors, the other two leaders feared for themselves and their families. Within the group of clan leaders and family members, there was some movement. Then a flash grenade rolled out of the crowd toward Raiden and detonated. The sound was so sharp, and the light blinding. Raiden could tell there was some movement. Ariel, Abban, the other warriors, and the sailors were all out of range to be in a full shock of the flash grenade, but still a little stunned by the sound and light. There were multiple footsteps heard running.

Once everything was fully clear, Raiden saw his niece running over to him. Arms wide open and ready to hug family again. The two embraced together, Jessica putting her head on Raiden's shoulders and crying. "I am sorry, I failed," Raiden whispered. His niece just laid her head on his shoulders. They both felt the pain and sorrow of the loss of the family, but joy and happiness also returned as they were together once again after a dreadful year.

"It isn't your fault". Jessica told Raiden. Hearing his niece say she didn't blame him lifted a boulder from Raiden's shoulders. "Thanks," He said in return. Feeling pain, self-hatred, self-blame, and other feelings of negativity leave his mind. He knew those thoughts may return at times, but with the love of his friends and wonderful niece, he could finally fight them off when needed.

Raiden looked over at the group of warriors, knights, serpents, and hawk clan family members kneeling on the stage in surrender, but where were the Charles of the lions clan, and where was the man who killed his family? They must have escaped during the blast. He was ready to bolt up in pursuit, but Ariel and Abban walked onto the stage, followed by Charles and the man who killed Raiden's family, with Mangus walking behind the two criminals with his axe ready for action.

Raiden and Jessica walked over to the Shairyn leader standing next to Charles. Once in front of the leader, with a strong, swift swing, Raiden punched the leader in the gut. The man gasped for air, and Raiden could tell he was in pain. Jessica followed Raiden's actions, grabbing the back of his shirt, holding him in a position as she slammed her knee in his face. The man dropped to the ground with a bloody nose. Once he was on the ground, both Jessica and Raiden started brutally kicking his body. Ariel ran over, pushing Raiden to the side and pulling Jessica away. "Enough!" She shouted. Raiden looked over at her with a furious face, but he agreed. He knew the punishment was later.

CHAPTER 51

"Take them out of here," Mangus commanded a group of thunder warriors while pointing at Charles and the Shairyn leader. He then pointed at the handful of Shairyn Knights. "Execute this scum." The large group of Raven, Crow, and Shamrock warriors opened fire on the Knights. The knights fell to the floor of the stage. Raiden watched as Mangus walked over to the other three traitor families. Raiden could tell that one leader of the two families was in his wife's hands, dead, and the other was wounded and being helped by other family members.

"Put Alvan with Charles," Mangus commanded. Five of the Raven warriors grabbed Alvan out of his family's hands and started to just drag him away. The group of family members cried out, "Please help him, he might die." The ravens did not pay any attention. Mangus just walked over and replied, "Good." The family looked shocked and a little angry.

"You are lucky," Mangus told the families. "We will spare you." They all looked surprised and happy, but simultaneously worried. "But I am banning you from Gateway and will take you to the forbidden lands," Mangus said. Some of the family members cried, and others made sounds of anger. To Mangus, it was only fair that these untitled families now pay the price for their actions against him and the other clans of Gateway. Warriors rounded up the group of family members and walked them off the stage. This was another remarkable story for the future children of Gateway about Gateway standing up against the Dynasty. With the traitors captured and the battle won, it was now time to celebrate their victory. Still in the back of Mangus's mind, he knew this would not be his last or Gateway's last conflict with the dynasty. There were future battles to fight. This was just the beginning of the war that the dynasty had created. And they would pay dearly for the mistake of starting this war, Mangus thought. But with the battle done and the city saved, it was time to celebrate. Mangus waved at one warrior. The warriors went to the Glass Tower, and only a minute later, there was music playing on speakers across the town. As loudly as possible for the city to hear, "Time to celebrate!" Mangus shouted out.

CHAPTER 52

That night, there was music across the city. The taverns overflowed with cheerful patrons. Mangus stood in front of the mead hall, a few blocks away from the Glass Tower. He took his full mug and swallowed all his ale. This was only the beginning for him. Mangus saw Raiden, Jessica, and Diego talking among themselves, holding their mugs.

Mangus walked over, putting down the mug he had and grabbing another one on the table. Mangus addressed them, saying,

"Well, my fellow warriors. What do you think of the celebration of Buaid?" Raiden had just learned what buaid meant, victory, from a conversation with Abban before he and Ariel had walked off to spend time together. Raiden could tell that after the battle was over, Ariel was interested in Abban. It thrilled Raiden to see Ariel for once, with a smile on her face. "It was amazing," Raiden replied to Mangus. Mangus raised his glass. "Skoal!" they all shouted.

As the night went by, everyone was drunker and drunker until people started to just pass out at the tables and chairs. "We should rest," Mangus told Raiden. Raiden and Mangus were some of the only people still awake. "See you in the morning, my fellow warrior." Mangus had not stopped calling Raiden, Diego, and Ariel warriors all night. It was a great compliment. Despite that, it was a little hard for Raiden to think of himself as a warrior. Many of the Warriors had called Raiden and his friends the Archangels, sometimes just as the angels. It was a new nickname after being called the bandits for so long. Mangus started with all his men to call the emperor of the Shairyn dynasty the devil. And gave Shoals of honor to Raiden, Ariel, Diego, and all the sailors multiple times that night to help free Gateway from the dynasty invasion. Raiden sat down in one chair and lowered his head onto his arms, resting on the top of the table. Falling asleep without a problem. For once, the dream of the night wasn't a nightmare, but a peaceful dream of joy.

Chapter 53

Raiden woke up to the sound of fellow warriors waking up and getting ready for the warrior's burial. Raiden got up and went to find Diego and Jessica. They were by the doorway outside. Diego was sitting up, leaning against the door frame, and Jessica was on her side on the floor with a blanket rolled up as her pillow. A few mugs were sitting around them, a couple still having ale in them.

Raiden gave Diego a little shove on the shoulders. It took a second, but Diego woke up with a face of pain, putting his head in his hands and making a moaning noise. Raiden figured it was Diego's first hangover. It made sense. The ale at this party was much stronger than what you could find in the flatlands.

Jessica woke up to Diego's moaning. As she was waking up, Raiden saw a scared face and depression in her eyes. But once her eyes were fully open and she was awake, Jessica noticed Raiden and smiled.

"Okay, in respect, we had better get to the ceremony." They all got up, wiped off some dust, and then walked to the river banks where the ceremony was. It was a small but cold shower that morning. As they walked through the city, they saw hundreds of people waking up who lay on the ground or slept while sitting up. The people all walked with them to the river in the rain. It turned into a heavy shower, and a gray day with no sun. Just dark gray clouds with a little thunder in the background. Gateway received significantly more rain than Raiden was accustomed to in the flatlands.

They followed the crowd with groups of people wearing different outfits. There were men wearing kilts and women wearing bright white dresses. Other men wearing the armor they had just fought in, with the blood of their enemy still on it. Along with some people dressed in old-style suits, the type that Raiden, Diego, and Ariel found in some of the ancient ruins. They sold that clothing for a good chunk of money to some people of the dynasty. In the Dynasty, only Nova's members and the upper class wore such suits.

They all walked down and out of the gate to the muddy river. Just outside the walls of Gateway, the crowd gathered at the edge of the river. The rain slowed down into more of a drizzle. On the back of a wagon on the riverbank, Mangus stood next to Abban. Behind them was a group of warriors wearing white armor with a small symbol on the chest, looking like a red cross. There were small bonfires behind the warriors, with dozens of little wooden boats with the bodies of the warriors, sailors, and citizens on them who had died during the battle.

"We lost many. But they all fought in honor. Saving Gateway. Their honor to fight is the reason for our survival."

Mangus raised his arm with his warrior axe in his hand. "In the name of these people, have the Doorway of Valhalla open in their honor." The group of armored men in white pushed the boats out on the mud river. They floated down the river. Mangus looked at Abban. Abban raised his Warhammer towards the sky. It lit up with a blue glow, and in seconds, there were veins of light flickering in the clouds, with a bolt slamming into the Warhammer. Abban swung the Warhammer down and aimed at the boats floating down the river. The bolt of lightning flew like a river of power from the sky to the Warhammer and then into the middle boat. The power is dispersed among all the boats, with bursts of flames lighting up on every boat.

The battle horns went off in a slow, soothing tune, turning into bagpipes, and the people of Gateway hummed along with the music. It had a peaceful and loving tune to it. A man the night before had talked about the music that would be played at the ceremony the next morning, called Amazing Grace. It was beautiful music with the feeling of strength and peace in it.

Once the music was over, the people all walked back into the city. The three walked over to talk to Mangus and Abban. The two stood looking over the river as the boats slowly went out of sight in the misty fog of the river. Ariel stood next to Abban, holding his hand. Raiden walked up to Ariel and asked, "How was your night?" Ariel just grinned in return and replied, "Magnificent, if you must know." Abban looked over and smiled. Mangus turned around and walked over to Raiden.

"How is my fellow warrior this morning?"

"I am good." Raiden replied, "Not so much for Diego. He has his first hangover." Raiden said with a little laugh.

Mangus looked at Diego with a grin. "It is just the beginning." He said.

EPILOGUE

Ariel and Diego sat on their horse, waiting for Jessica and Raiden to get out of the Glass tower and start heading home with them. It had been a great 3 months since the battle. There was a statue being made to be put in the town square of what the sculptor called the Archangels of Gateway. It was a group of figures dressed and armored for battle. But each figure of the group was a sculptor of each member of the sailors who fought, along with the ones who had fallen, and Ariel, Diego, and Raiden. According to the people of Gateway, Ariel, Diego, and Raiden were no longer just the bandits, but were now the Archangels of Gateway. Now and forever, Gateway welcomed Ariel, Diego, and Raiden.

Raiden and Jessica walked out of the Tower with smiles on their faces. Jessica was even giggling a little. Reminding Raiden that she was a young adult or not, Jessica was still just a kid to him, his little niece. Behind them were Mangus and Abben, walking with them to their horses. Raiden and Jessica got on their horses.

"You sure you don't need me?" Mangus asked.

"We're good, but thanks," Raiden replied.

"Get hold of us if you need help," Mangus told Raiden. "Or to party." Abban continued, giving Ariel a smile. Raiden now saw life in Ariel's eyes. After her mission with Abban and spending the last three months with him, Ariel looked happier than ever before. The last three months had been wonderful for her, Raiden thought. He still wondered why Ariel, with no solid ties to Sand Town besides her friends, hadn't stayed longer at Gateway with Abban. It was easy for everyone else to tell that they were in love, but she insisted she was fine and that going back to Sand Town without Abban was ok. The four turned their horses around and started down the road.

As they walked out of the city and crossed the bridge that covered the muddy river, they saw the pillars with the three bodies on them. After three months, there were now just skeletons of Alvin and Blake. Guards had kept them chained to poles in the town square for two weeks. The people of Gateway would walk by them and spit on them. Every morning, the businesses of the town would have the water they used to mop or wash anything dumped on top of the two. Citizens gave them only scraps or garbage to eat, and other citizens' dogs ate the food intended for them. By the end of the second week, Mangus and the other clan leaders mercifully executed them, as they were nearly starving to death. Stabbed and left to bleed to death, tied to the pillars outside of town in front of the bridge. Even with all the chaos that was caused and the traitors they were, tied and left to bleed to death, it was still cruel in Raiden's mind. Unlike the traitor clan leaders, whom the public had mercy on for two weeks, Raiden, the leader of the dynasty warriors, took Mangus in for interrogation.

Lucifer had been a stubborn, loyal Shairyn soldier. He had broken legs and a broken arm, but when Mangus ordered him to lose his manhood, Lucifer's defense crumbled. But even after giving all the information on what clans besides just the Hawks and Serpents collaborated with Charles, and the names of any business people or supporters of the three traitor clans. Mangus found that more business people supported the takeover of Gateway than Mangus had expected. Most of the supporters of the takeover fled town when the battle started. Guards caught only a dozen and took them to the prison south of town, placing them with any surviving lion, hawk, and serpent warriors.

Farmers used the prisoners as slave labor during harvest, and authorities used them for other manual labor throughout the year when necessary; otherwise, the prisoners remained locked in their cells.

Even though Lucifer disclosed the information, they still emasculated him. Unlike the traitors, they enslaved Lucifer, but this time for the city itself. They assigned Lucifer to clean sewage pipes and remove any horse and cattle dung found in town. He was a slave for life with no chance of freedom, even if he served in a battle on behalf of Gateway. To Raiden, it was a good punishment. Raiden knew that punishment would not make the pain go away. Making it so that Lucifer suffering the rest of his life would have to do for Raiden.

Raiden shook his head to clear it for the moment, to see where they were now. He could tell that it had been an hour or more since leaving Gateway. Raiden found they were at the crossing into officially Shairyn Dynasty land, and there stood a sign showing the arsenal, two hundred miles north. It was time to head home, Raiden thought to himself.

THE END

PLEASE LEAVE A REVIEW

AND LET US KNOW WHAT YOU THINK

Acknowledgments

J.C. Juhl would like to thank his family for their support on his journey as

an author. His wife's and daughter's support were instrumental in

igniting his drive to become a published author.

He would also like to thank his colleagues from the

Eastern Iowa Writers Guild,

His English teacher Dianne Pichard,

Kirkwood Community College,

Support staff such as

ITP: Sarah, Amy, Peggy, Tessa, Ariel, Chuck

BV: Josh-SOAS: Shawn

J.C. Juhl would also like to shout out to

Writing Excuses, Brandon Sanderson, Jenna Moreci, and Bethany

Atazadeh, for the education they provide in becoming an author.

J.C. JUHL

About the Author

J.C. Juhl is an author of science fiction, with thrills and adventure as a core and a side of Mystery added. J.C. Juhl lives in a rural town surrounded by corn and soybean fields as far as the eye can see. J.C. Juhl lives with his loving family and furry friends, Louie, Mario (Dogs), Leo, and Nova (Cats). He is a Geek, a fan of comic books, DC and Marvel Movies/Shows, Netflix and YouTube

Remember to leave a review.

And tell us

What do you think of the story?

J.C. JUHL

J.C. JUHL